He's the One

Look for these titles by
Jane Beckenham

Now Available:

Romeo for Hire
Secrets and Seduction

He's the One

Jane Beckenham

Samhain Publishing, Ltd.
577 Mulberry Street, Suite 1520
Macon, GA 31201
www.samhainpublishing.com

He's the One
Copyright © 2011 by Jane Beckenham
Print ISBN: 978-1-60928-074-1
Digital ISBN: 978-1-60928-040-6

Editing by Linda Ingmanson
Cover by Scott Carpenter

This book is a work of fiction. The names, characters, places, and incidents are products of the writer's imagination or have been used fictitiously and are not to be construed as real. Any resemblance to persons, living or dead, actual events, locale or organizations is entirely coincidental.

All Rights Are Reserved. No part of this book may be used or reproduced in any manner whatsoever without written permission, except in the case of brief quotations embodied in critical articles and reviews.

This book has been previously published.
First Samhain Publishing, Ltd. electronic publication: May 2010
First Samhain Publishing, Ltd. print publication: March 2011

Dedication

To every writer I know who has the grit and determination to keep on going, I take my hat off to you!

Chapter One

"Virginity is overrated." Easy words? She'd said them often enough.

Yet when Taylor Sullivan whispered them, the swell of panic threatened to take hold.

She had to do this.

It was time.

Taylor exhaled every emotion she'd bottled for the past twenty-four hours, ever since she'd seen him: Mr. Perfect-for-the-Job.

As she stood outside the bar, her bravado waned and panic set in. Who wouldn't panic when they were about to make an off-the-wall suggestion to a stranger?

She gripped her assistant's arm. "I can't. This is a mistake."

"No, it's not. You said so yourself, he's the one."

"What do I know? I mean, *who* is he?"

"Cade Harper. Bad boy made good—and one sexy hunk. Is that enough for you?" Nita gave her a suggestive grin.

Oh, yeah.

Taylor wiped her sweaty palms down the sides of her skirt. "The fairy godmother sure did hand out good looks at his bassinet." He'd been the best man at a wedding she'd planned recently. Haloed by the light streaming in from the stained glass window, he'd taken her breath away.

But now, twenty-four hours after that wedding, as the throbbing beat of music threaded its way out onto the kerb where she and Nita waited, Taylor's wayward nerves vaulted into overdrive. "I should never have told you."

Nita shrugged. "Probably not, but, hey, I get those calls too."

"But you can answer them," Taylor countered.

"So, what are you going to do about it?"

Taylor bit down on her bottom lip, chewing it as if it afforded her the luxury of time. "I don't want a relationship."

"Who said anything about a relationship? This is a fling. A one-nighter. Get you past first base, so to speak."

First base! Taylor swallowed the lump that choked off her breathing. The icy chill sliding along her bones had absolutely nothing to do with Auckland's balmy May evening breeze.

Her fingers grazed the side of her handbag and snapped back as if scalded when she remembered exactly what her bag contained.

Condoms!

An appropriate reminder: preparation and safety first.

She could do this. She could. She grabbed Nita's arm. "Okay. Let's go."

Nita stalled mid-step. "What? You expect me to come too?"

"I need you. I can't do this on my own. I need..."

"Cade Harper is who you need, Taylor. You said so yourself. Cade's a love 'em and leave 'em sort of guy. Now go." Nita gave her a push toward the entrance and waved goodbye.

Love and leave. Definitely perfect credentials. Cade didn't know it yet, but he was the answer to Taylor's prayers.

He's the One

Battling the raw panic lodged in her gut as every second edged her toward turning and running, Taylor surveyed the patrons. Her hands shook. She wanted to forget the idea. Forget sex. Forget Cade Harper. If she could.

Instead she focused on the entrance, and her pulse quickened.

The best man. How appropriate.

Cade hadn't been at the wedding rehearsal; otherwise she would have noticed him. But at the wedding, dressed in a black tuxedo that molded his broad shoulders and a crisp white dress shirt with diamond stud buttons, he absolutely stood out and, within seconds, she'd made her decision. He was perfect for the job.

Squaring her shoulders, Taylor shoved the bar door open. For a moment, she stood motionless, eyes adjusting to the dim lighting, the noise and heat hitting her in an undulating wave.

This was it.

Taking a deep breath, she clutched her bag and ventured in.

A single length of hand-chiseled wood operated as a bar and spanned one end of the room. Behind it were a medley of liquors and an ornate mirror etched with the slogan of a famous beer. Tables and chairs dotted around the room were mostly already taken. In one corner, a jukebox emitted ear-piercing rock music, while in another corner, an eager group of players surrounded a pool table.

All of this was of little consequence to Taylor, because all she could focus on was her quarry—Cade Harper.

He stood behind the bar, a cocktail shaker in one hand and a salt-crusted margarita glass in the other.

Tawny, sun-bronzed hair tapered over his collar, and an unruly tendril dipped across his forehead, seemingly refusing to

11

be controlled. He looked good. Very sexy.

No tuxedo tonight, but a black T-shirt with the sleeves rolled back, stretched taut over biceps that flexed and...

Oh, God.

Definitely a bad boy.

Taylor wiped a hand across her brow and her tongue over suddenly parched lips. The temperature had escalated several degrees in one blazing second.

Partially hidden by a potted ficus, heart dancing an erratic beat, she watched Cade.

"Can I help you?"

Taylor spun around. "I..."

The voice belonged to a female version of Cade. She had the same coloring and the same dark eyes. Taylor glanced toward Cade over the woman's head. "I'm here to see Mr. Harper," she mumbled. *Mister! Good grief!* She wanted to have sex with this man, and she called him mister!

"Cade?" his replica responded, eyebrows quirking upward.

Taylor nodded, relieved the woman didn't ask any questions, and wondered at the same time what her reaction would have been if she'd said, "It's about sex."

"Follow me." The young woman crooked her finger toward Taylor, turned and wove her way between tables. With trepidation and anticipation colliding inside her stomach, Taylor hurried after her.

"Cade."

"Yeah." He handed the margarita to a customer, and Taylor's gaze followed the salt-rimmed glass. It shimmered under the overhead lighting, and she found herself licking her lips, almost tasting the delicious salt.

"Lady to see you."

The moment Cade turned, *everything* changed.

Cade Harper. Bad boy. One sexy guy.

Taylor's voice stalled in her throat, and she knew, when his smiling eyes captured hers, she was in way over her head.

Cade wiped his hands on a cloth and again Taylor's gaze followed. Long, lean fingers. Fingers that would touch... *Oh, boy!*

He smiled. "You wanted to see me?"

She nodded and felt herself drowning in that smile. His dark eyes twinkled, a swirl of gold and chocolate brown. Just like Hershey Kisses.

Kisses!

Yep. She was definitely going under.

"Lady, I don't mean to be rude, but I've got a bar to run," he said, grabbing a knife and cutting a lemon into wafer-thin slices.

Taylor shook herself. *Okay. Come on. Just say it.* "I've got a favor to ask."

"Ask away then," he said, not looking up.

Taylor burned and eyed the milling crowd. "Actually, it's a proposition."

He definitely looked then, and his gaze focused on her. He placed the razor-sharp knife on the cutting board. His mouth quirked at one corner, smiling, gaze assessing. "Sounds intriguing."

Sounds stupid.

He leant forward and rested both hands on the bar, the flex and tension in his forearms a powerful tease. Taylor swallowed hard.

"Is there anywhere we can talk—privately?"

"Out back in the den." He flicked a hand toward a door behind the bar.

"More like going into the lion's den," she muttered.

"You say something?"

"Ah...no." She dropped her gaze. Damn. Why hadn't she chosen a different career? One where her clients didn't ask about sex?

Holding herself stiff and feeling as if all eyes followed her movements, she walked behind the bar. As she brushed past him, the musky scent of his cologne teased her senses. Taylor willed the butterflies dancing a tango in her stomach to abate. They didn't listen.

No more than a storeroom with boxes piled high along three of its four walls and a desk barely visible beneath a pile of papers and computer sheets, this room wore many different hats.

Every word Taylor had practiced dissolved from her memory as Cade closed the door behind him. The soft click of the latch echoed a thousand-fold. She spun around. He leant against the door, arms folded across his formidable chest, his gaze candid. He looked dangerous—but very delicious.

He spoke first. "Do I know you?"

"Not really." *Not yet.*

"Shame." He gave another of his long, lingering smiles, the kind that emphasized the dimples on either side of his sexy mouth. It set her toes curling and her body pulsing. Her internal temperature gauge hit the jackpot. Oh, Lordy, she was out of her depth.

But here goes.

"I'm Taylor Sullivan. We didn't meet, exactly, at Brianna Bennett's wedding. I was her planner." She jerked out her hand.

Cade took it in his. Warm, strong fingers enveloped hers. The tips were slightly calloused, and the friction sent goose bumps skittering across her heated skin. She willed herself not to yank her hand from his and held herself in check.

"You touting for another wedding to plan?" Cade pushed away from the door, dwarfing the room. He shoved his hands deep into the pockets of jeans that skimmed his long, muscular thighs. "If you are," he said, with a shrug, "you're out of luck. Marriage and I don't mix."

Taylor tightened her grip on her bag, desperate to silence the slamming of her heartbeat. "So I heard."

"You've heard more about me than I have of you," he replied.

A hint of a smile tipped the corners of her mouth. "You're quite well known, Mr. Harper. Successful and entrepreneurial."

"I work hard."

"And play hard, so the papers say."

"Gossip and innuendo," he countered, his steely gaze sizing her up.

A bead of sweat trickled between her breasts. Cade hadn't taken his eyes off her since they'd entered the back room.

That has to be a good thing. Shows he's interested, her subconscious reminded her.

Taylor shifted from foot to foot.

It's now or never, Sullivan.

With a deep breath that really didn't soothe her chaotic thoughts, she pulled herself to her full five-foot-ten height and dived in. "I want you to have sex with me."

Cade's dark eyes bolted wide. "Whoa."

Heat suffused Taylor's cheeks. "Oh, hell, this is stupid." How dumb could she be? She reached for her bag, but the overladen carryall slid from her fingers and upended, scattering its contents across the floor.

Taylor gasped and, for one long, drawn-out second, simply stared. Her breath strangulated in her throat, and a furious heat burned behind her eyes. There, right at Cade's feet, lay her box of condoms.

Blinking back tears, she dropped to her knees and gathered everything as fast as she could. "Stupid, stupid."

Then worse worsened.

Cade reached the condoms the second before she did.

"You must be a good Girl Scout," he said and passed the box to her.

Their fingers touched.

Their eyes met.

Held.

All the oxygen seemed to be sucked from her lungs. She pulled away, shaking her head, struggling for a semblance of practicality.

"Always be prepared. Isn't that their motto?" Cade chuckled.

This was bad. Really bad. Mortified, Taylor refused to look at him and kept her lips firmly closed. She shoved the box into her bag and zipped it closed with a firm tug.

Open up again, she warned silently, *and you'll be in the rubbish bin.*

She straightened, walked to the door and opened it. Strains of Dr. Hook's "Sexy Eyes" wafted into the small room. How appropriate. Cade's dark eyes were just that, downright sinful and sexy.

"Wait," he said.

"Why?"

"You've just proposed something way out there and I want to know why."

Her hand fell from the door.

"You intrigue me." Cade's seductive gaze traveled her length, lighting a trail of heat to the tips of her toes. "Are you going to tell me why you walked in here and offered yourself? Sex is a serious game."

Taylor searched for the right words, unsure if there were any right ones. "In my business, I need experience."

"You plan weddings. You don't have to sleep with the grooms."

Taylor gasped, but not one single word came out. Cade wanted an answer. Deserved one. She clutched her bag, kneading the leather. "I...get asked questions," she finally managed to whisper.

"What sort of questions?"

"Damn it, Cade, do I have to spell it out?"

"Seems so," he said with a hint of amusement glittering in his way-too-sexy eyes.

"You're enjoying this."

"Sure," he said, not even denying it. He gave another of his smiles, the ones that got her all hot and bothered. And right now, she was *very* bothered.

"I get asked questions—about sex. S-E-X. Got it?" Taylor looked everywhere but at Cade.

"Got it."

She thought he'd laugh, joke, something, but not do this...not be gentle. Cade caught her chin in his fingers, turning her so she had to look at him. "So why not answer them?"

Oh, man. Where were those damned red shoes of Dorothy's when she needed them? Kansas looked pretty appealing right now.

"I can't answer them."

"Can't?"

The tip of her tongue slid along her teeth. "Look, I realize this is on the edge of weird."

"True," he agreed, much to her chagrin. "I don't have a beautiful lady come into my bar every day and ask for sex."

He didn't? Taylor's brows knitted. Why not? Cade was hunk material. He made her forget—everything.

"Questions," he prompted.

Oh, God, there was no way out. Not even an earthquake could save her now. "The questions are something that goes with the territory of being a wedding planner. Brides get anxious," she said, hugging her bag to her chest. "They may be experienced, even living with their partners, but sometimes, as the wedding draws near, they get skittery. They ask, um...questions—about sex. Questions I can't answer, because..."

"Because you're a virgin?"

Oh, where was that earthquake when a girl wanted it? "That's right." Heat burned her face. Her scalp. Everywhere. She speared Cade with a direct glare. *Don't you dare laugh! Don't you make me feel any worse than I do*, she silently challenged.

But he didn't laugh. He didn't smile. What he did was worse. Much worse.

He closed the gap between them. Taylor's body erupted into high alert, nipples pebbling beneath her lacy bra. She could deal with him at a distance. But close up, everything changed. Body heat got in the way.

Taylor Sullivan certainly captured his attention. She wanted sex with him. And that sounded great.

Bemused, Cade stared down into eyes the color of a field of cornflowers beneath a wide blue sky. The kind of eyes that made him feel she could see deep into his soul, understand things he didn't want her to know. Things he hid, even from himself. All this from one moment in time.

He blinked.

What the hell was wrong with him? Thank God he'd kept those thoughts to himself.

"Most women who come in here asking for sex are..."

"Party girls," she offered.

Cade watched her bite at her bottom lip. "I should say no. It's a wild scheme."

"So why don't you?"

Yeah, why not, Cade?

With her hair caught up in a sleek chignon and the prim and proper clothes she wore, no hint of skin peeking out anywhere, it was as if she tried to hide the real woman. Taylor in no way exemplified how he thought a wedding planner would look.

Then she smiled at him, and all thoughts of a prim little miss vanished. He realized, with the shock of a man used to making solid, sensible business decisions, he found himself actually considering her offer.

In the past, plenty of women wanted him, but he preferred to do the chasing.

"You're not really my type." *Who's lying now, Harper?*

"So what is your type? A woman in shorts and a tube top

with an empty space for a brain?"

"Meow," he chided. "Not nice."

A soft pink flush colored her cheeks. He liked that. Showed she wasn't as hard as she made herself out to be. A point in her favor.

"I'm sorry."

"That's okay. I figure it took a lot of guts for you to walk in here. What I can't figure out is why me? There are plenty of guys out there who'd take you up on your offer."

"Perhaps," she acquiesced, wiping the tip of her tongue across her bottom lip, an action Cade found himself following in minute detail. Damn it. He was hooked, and his arousal had made itself blatantly obvious and him uncomfortable. Embarrassed to be caught like a schoolboy in heat, he moved to sit behind his desk.

"You're renowned for the parade of women you leave behind."

His rumbling laughter filled the room. "You've done your homework."

"I'm a businesswoman. I know my business."

"And sex is your business?"

"No!"

He could see he'd shocked her. Her eyes widened like saucers, all glistening and...innocent. Cade's groin tightened. Such a tempting proposal.

Taylor continued. "Weddings, love and commitment are my business."

"Yet you searched me out knowing commitment is definitely not my middle name."

"That's *exactly* why I chose you. You don't believe in everlasting love or roses and the white picket fence deal."

"For others, maybe, but not for me," he agreed. "But you, Taylor, are a wedding planner. You've got to be a romantic at heart."

"I'm a businesswoman," she reiterated. "Marriage is a good business."

"And yet you haven't married."

Taylor shrugged, but she couldn't hide the shadow of sadness that washed across her eyes before the fall of her heavy lashes blotted it out.

"So now we get back to my commitment, or lack of it," Cade said.

Taylor fixed her steadfast blue eyes on him. "Mr. Harper, I don't want commitment, either. So we're a good match. *And* I have a deal for you."

Cade's eyebrows quirked upward. "This gets more interesting by the minute. But maybe you should try Cade. It's less formal, since we'll be getting to know each other...intimately."

Taylor choked back a cough. She twisted her shaking hands behind her back and linked her fingers. Her chin lifted a fraction. "I understand you're looking at expanding the chain and starting up more of a boutique line of cocktail bars."

"I'm surprised you found that out. It hasn't been advertised."

"I told you, I'm a..."

"Businesswoman. Yeah. I know. Very impressive. So, what's the deal?"

"You want to expand your empire, to expose yourself."

Cade chuckled. "Sounds provocative."

"I...didn't mean the way it sounded."

"I know, just teasing. Sorry, you were offering me a sweetener to this proposal of yours." He folded his arms across his chest, which did nothing for Taylor's equilibrium as she eyed the play of his T-shirt over taut muscles.

She breathed. Deeply. And again, and again, trying to remain calm. "I know promotions," she said. "I'll promote your new venture, for...ah..."

"Services rendered," he offered.

Her lips pursed. "Something like that."

Cade pushed himself from his desk and stood in front of her. His gaze dropped to her face, and he cupped her chin, thumb circling her cheek. His touch felt so soft and so gentle, she almost purred.

"I'm definitely interested. But let's get this straight. You use your promotional skills in return for my lovemaking skills?"

Taylor's breath whooshed out in a sharp exhalation. Oh, Lord. It sounded brazen and so not her. Again she wondered what on earth she was doing.

Getting in too deep without a lifejacket, that's what.

But Cade had agreed, and now she had to close the deal. "There's just one thing," she said, aware as her body tilted forward, anticipation zinging through her veins.

"Another request?" Cade's eyes narrowed, suspicion and an almost jaundiced expectation flickering across his face. He shrugged. "Okay, shoot."

"Well, I need you to kiss me."

Chapter Two

"Easy request." Cade's mouth quirked to one side and Taylor found herself focusing on his dimples—again. "It'd be my pleasure," he added.

Pleasure. Lordy. Lordy. Lordy. The word rolled off the tip of his tongue as if simply saying it invoked what he wanted to do to her. The thought sent a shivery heat skimming across her skin.

"Any particular type of kiss?"

Oh, hell.

"A peck on the cheek, or the full Monty?"

Double hell.

Her body hummed with expectation, senses firing on all cylinders. Barely inches from him, she searched his face. No mirth. Instead, scalding lust shone in Cade's gaze, promising everything.

Then his lips were on hers, and Taylor couldn't tell if she'd acted first or if he did. Just that he tasted warm and soft. And delicious.

He laced one hand through her hair and gently tugged at the pins holding it in place, tossing them aside. The soft ping as they hit the floor was inaudible compared to the roar of her heartbeat. As her hair cascaded in a silken veil, Cade cupped her face, one thumb teasing the curve of her jaw.

He moaned his pleasure. Taylor's stomach clenched. Her eyes closed, and she shifted closer to him, coming to rest against the apex of his long legs. She wanted more, needed to touch him. She linked her hands around his neck, feeling the sinewy flex of his muscles. Her fingertips brushed against his hair—a thousand electric volts washing over every sensitive cell of her skin.

"You feel so good," he murmured against her mouth.

Cade's husky drawl slipped between them and sliced her fantasy in two. She stilled. Her fingers arrested their exploratory dance and pushed him away. "We can't. Not here."

"We just did."

Taylor lifted her gaze and looked at him. How could he remain so calm and collected while she struggled for a semblance of propriety? She tugged at her clothes, but her hands shook and nothing seemed to work. She wished she were anywhere but here.

"There are people just through that door," she said, looking over her shoulder. "Anyone could walk in."

"We could lock the door."

Taylor's blood sizzled. "You've caught me off-guard."

He stared down into her eyes, searching as if he wanted to see every part of her. "What did you expect? You come waltzing into my bar with some concocted scheme and then ask for a kiss. Was it some sort of test?"

Taylor's mind raced with so many thoughts she couldn't make sense of anything. All she could focus on was the taste of Cade on her lips.

"You wanted to test the goods first. You got it." He paced the small room, then abruptly turned and rested his large frame against the desk. He folded his arms across his chest. Big and powerful. And definitely sexy as sin.

Suddenly, sin seemed enticing.

"Well?"

"There has to be some spark, doesn't there?" Taylor challenged weakly.

"Spark?" Cade cursed. He dragged a hand through his unruly hair. "If you felt the full force of my spark, sweetheart, you'd run a mile."

"I would not."

"Hell, you would. That spark was...hot, damn it."

"Look, I think I should go." *See, you are running.* Taylor ignored her subconscious. "This is a bad idea." She gathered up her bag—carefully, this time. "I'm sorry."

She sucked in a deep breath, steeling herself for the crowd outside, and nodded curtly at Cade. "Goodbye."

"Where are you going?" Cade's sharp tone brought her to a halt, and she shot him a "what do you care" look over her shoulder.

"Home."

"How?"

"I'll call a cab."

But before she had a chance to stall him, Cade snatched up keys from his desk. "I'll take you."

She gripped the door, knuckles bleached of color. "I'd prefer a cab, thank you. Besides, aren't you working?"

"I'm the owner. I can play hooky." He dangled the keys. "No tricks. Gentleman's honor." And he crossed his heart.

Taylor went to speak, but he silenced her with the tip of his finger resting against her parted lips.

Heat zinged between them, and Taylor had the distinct urge to wrap her tongue around it. To suck it. Very blatantly. Sexually.

"Don't argue, Ms. Sullivan." He gave her a sheepish grin that did more to her equilibrium than Taylor wanted to admit. "Mind you, we could call it our first lovers' tiff."

"Lovers?" She exhaled and went limp against him.

The flat of his hand palmed the small of her back, and with the other he switched off the light. Darkness encircled them, a sweet relief from his knowing gaze. She could feel his heat, hear the rampaging beat of her heart behind her ribs.

"You put some crazy proposition to me tonight, Taylor, and, damn it, I have no idea why, but let's just say you've got a date."

Oh, boy.

"A date." Those two words sounded extraordinarily provocative.

He opened the door and stood back as she walked past him. Through the bar, he walked beside her. Taylor's emotions were frayed. She couldn't even look at him. He called out to the young woman at the bar and gave her a wave. "Hey, sis, gotta go somewhere."

"Who's the lady, Cade?" came a shout from the direction of the pool table.

"Never you mind, Harry. Keep your mitts off."

A raucous hoot of laughter rippled around the room. "I think our Cade's found himself a hot chick."

"'Bout time," called another.

Cade waved the crowd off and directed Taylor toward the exit, the pressure of his hand increasing.

She couldn't get out of there fast enough, and the moment

they walked through the exit, she breathed a sigh of relief.

His expression was apologetic. "Sorry about that. It's football night. The guys are celebrating a win by the local footie team."

"You seem to know everyone," she said as she walked at his side.

"Goes with the territory. The more you get to know your customers, the better business is. They think you're interested in their lives, so they feel at home. And if they feel comfortable, then they're likely to spend more."

"Makes sense."

"Yeah, it does. But damned if this does." He frowned and shoved his hands deep into the pockets of his jeans. Taylor followed his movements, and her eyes widened as she saw what his tight jeans emphasized. She slid her tongue over her lips as a wave of panic washed through her.

"You don't have to do this," she said.

"Don't I?"

"No," she said, but she couldn't stall the sense of disappointment she'd feel if Cade changed his mind. "Look, I'll help you with your business. It doesn't matter about the...ah...other thing."

"The virginity thing?"

Taylor swallowed hard. Why hadn't she done something about this a long time ago? But she knew why. Her life had been hijacked.

They turned the corner and wove their way through the rows of cars before coming to a halt beside a sleek classic car.

A gasp of surprise flew from her lips. "This Mustang is *yours*?" She reached out to the car. It stood alone under the streetlight, beautiful, elegant, charged.

"Sure is."

She heard the unmistakable admiration and joy in Cade's acknowledgement and noticed the way his hands caressed the car's sleek curves. She dragged her gaze away, wanting to disown her thoughts. Trouble was, they ignited imagery as if the car's curves were *hers*. Skin against skin. Cade next to her. Hot, sleek and very tempting.

"Impressive. '64 Mustang, eight cylinder, isn't it?"

"You know cars?"

A soft flutter of laughter broke the hush. "Don't sound so surprised. Women can be into cars just as much as men."

"I know. I just didn't expect it."

"Why? Don't I look like a petrol head?"

"No, more like a prim little nun. A good girl." He looked at her then. Really looked. Slowly and deliberately. His hands slid through her hair. Such a sensual act. She held her breath.

She wondered what Cade saw. The real her? Or the sensible girl, the façade she enacted for everyone, including her family. Had he been able to see through her? Did she want him to?

Without speaking, Cade opened the car door, and she slid in, careful not to get too close. However, once seated, Taylor wasn't so sure if accepting his offer had been a good idea. The interior was small and far too intimate and only served to fire her wayward hormones.

In clipped tones, she gave him her address then retreated into silence.

As the car eased out of the car park, excitement, fear and anticipation all rolled into one coursed through her veins. It forced Taylor to focus on emotions she'd never experienced before, and she felt totally inadequate. Nothing in her life had prepared her for Cade. Being engaged to Rob held nothing to being taken for a ride by Cade.

And therein lay her problem.

"So how come wedding planning? Don't the couple and their families do that?" Cade asked as they drove through the silent suburb.

Her tension eased with a sigh of relief. This was her forte, and at last she could relax. "In the past, yes. But today people want something different."

"And you can give it to them?" he asked. Although Cade drove, Taylor read the true interest in his expression. She smiled and then chuckled.

"What?" He gave her a comical expression. "What did I say wrong?"

"Nothing. It's just the same expression I've seen many times before. The grooms would be happy with a tent and a few beers, then the bride gets some ideas, and it's never the same again. Horrified groom versus excited bride."

"So what do you do?"

"Dr. Phil says, 'If the wife ain't happy, then neither will anyone else be'. So seems to me there's a bit of meeting in the middle to get it sorted."

Cade looked suitably appalled, then refocused on the road. "And does it? Get sorted, I mean."

"Mostly."

"So what sort of weddings, besides expensive, do you conjure up for happy couples?"

"Fantasy, of course," she said proudly. "I create fantasies and give the couple the dream wedding they've always wanted."

Cade brought the Mustang to a halt right outside her house. The nightlight switched on automatically. Taylor frowned. No necking on the doorstep. She'd have to get rid of that light first thing in the morning.

He switched off the engine, and suddenly everything was silent.

"What about your dreams, Taylor?"

Her stomach clenched. "I haven't got any."

"None?"

"No." Not anymore. She wouldn't allow herself to dream and, uncomfortable with his questioning, she stared out the window at the night.

"Why Devonport?" Cade asked, looking around at the villas that typified the suburb.

"I like the close-knit community it offers. It's one of the oldest suburbs, so a sense of unity has built up over many years."

"Not afraid of the ghost on Mt. Victoria?"

"Never seen it, so how can I be afraid of it?"

"But you're afraid of me," he stated.

Taylor looked at him. Was she? She eyed his strong hands. She'd already felt their touch, knew what they could do to her. She imagined them touching her again. Everywhere. "No, I'm not afraid of you, Cade. Only of what I don't know."

"And you think you know me?"

"Enough," she said succinctly.

"Enough to trust me?"

Taylor hesitated. "Not quite," she admitted, then smiled a little shyly.

"That's good."

"I'm sorry if I put you on the spot tonight."

"Don't worry about it."

"So you get propositioned all the time?"

Cade shrugged. "Goes with the job."

She unlocked the door and pushed it open.

"One more thing." Cade's hand touched her bare shoulder. Sparks flew and her breath stalled in her lungs. She turned back to him, but when he cupped her face in an almost tender embrace, that gentleness sucked everything from her.

Then he kissed her.

Taylor gasped and inhaled his scent. Pure sex. Pure male. It almost sent her over the edge, to a place she hadn't known about. Till now.

She kissed him back.

He teased her mouth, grazing her bottom lip with the scrape of his teeth and, once again, Taylor began to drown.

"You can't bury yourself in your fantasy weddings, Taylor." His voice almost purred against her cheek.

But Taylor's brain had shut down to everything but the taste of him and the aching need that swelled deep inside her.

"This is our fantasy. Is this what you want?" he asked.

Definitely. But she didn't say so. She couldn't admit it. Not out loud. Not even to herself, really. She pulled away and grappled for oxygen. She needed to breathe. But, oh, how she needed Cade's kiss to go on forever.

Nothing is forever.

With shaking fingers, she battled for control, fumbling in her purse. She refused to look at the condoms. "Here's my card. If you..."

"I haven't changed my mind." He looked at her, dark eyes earnest. "It's still yes."

The card slipped from her fingers. "It is?"

"Uh-huh. So what's next?"

"I don't know."

"It's your call. You're the boss. Or did you think you'd just jump my bones and get it over with tonight?"

Taylor swallowed her embarrassment. Yes, that was exactly what she'd thought. Businesslike. Organized. Get it over with and get on with life.

He lifted her hand, turning it over as if trying to read her palm. He smiled—slow and sweet. It made her want to reach up and trace his mouth, to *feel* his smile.

"Sorry, no can do."

"Why not?" God, did she actually ask that?

"Because, call me old fashioned, but I think we need to take it slow, let it smolder, heat up and get us in the mood. Making love isn't 'wham bam thank you ma'am'. It's an art form."

Mood? An art form? Lord. She was in the mood *now*. One kiss and her body burned for him. She had to get out of here before she did exactly what he said and jumped his bones.

"Well, thank you for being a...gentleman."

"No problem. When would you like to meet again?"

How about ten minutes time, her subconscious offered.

"Um...maybe tomorrow. I've got to check my diary."

"Of course. Business before pleasure."

Taylor's head jerked up. She caught Cade's amused grin. Those dimples sure were a temptation.

"Business is what pays the bills."

"And love is what the makes the world go 'round, or so they say."

"This isn't about love."

Cade's grin slipped. "No, it's not. It's about giving you some experience. Don't worry. I'll phone you."

Taylor realized she'd been summarily dismissed. Thrusting open the car door, she jackknifed out as fast as her trembling legs allowed and, although she bent down to say thanks, Cade didn't give her time. He gunned his hot car and, with a squeal of tires, sped off into the night.

"Just like a knight in shining armor," Taylor murmured as she watched the retreating vehicle.

Trouble was, she wasn't sure she could handle being rescued by Mr. Harper.

The Mustang's revs vibrated as Cade drove up Mt. Victoria. He didn't have a clue why he headed there, except he wasn't ready to go back to the bar and face the curious glances or his sister's interrogation. Katie may have been the youngest of the Harper siblings, but she sure made up for it with her mothering. He'd got used to it over the years, but right now, he wasn't in the mood.

What he *was* in the mood for was Taylor Sullivan. Prim, uptight Taylor with long, slender legs he was sure went on forever. He imagined them wrapped around him, holding him to her.

And ankles... Since when had ankles become so darned sexy? Cade shifted uncomfortably. He needed a cold shower— and soon.

He couldn't help but wonder, though, what lay beneath her prim exterior. Didn't she know covering up was *way* more seductive? It left a guy wondering, and he sure did wonder.

He brought the car to a halt at the summit and cut the engine. Silence surrounded him while in the distance the city pulsed, the same way his body pulsed the moment he'd set eyes on Taylor. Unbuckling his seatbelt, he sank down on the seat, shutting out the lights below. But he couldn't shut out Taylor.

Her image replayed in his brain. Her soulful eyes, the way she looked at him, a soft wordless plea in a sea of blue that threatened to swamp him.

Better get your control back, Harper.

The way she blushed and looked away embarrassed, as if caught doing something naughty. Right now, naughty seemed very nice. And yet Cade had witnessed the desperation in her eyes too. Taylor wanted sexual experience, believing she would be able to better advise her clients. It sounded weird, but he could actually understand it. How often had he ended up as an unpaid counselor to a patron who cried into his drink?

Yeah, but you don't kiss them, don't undress them...and take them to bed.

And that was *his* problem. She'd asked him to kiss her. He'd done it and wanted more. Lots of it. Her lips, her body. Everything. One taste, one touch of her sweet and tempting mouth beneath his, and he'd been hooked.

"Dumb move, Harper."

He should have sent her packing. But he hadn't, and damn it, it felt right—when he knew it shouldn't. She was too— perfect. And that scared him. All he could think about was Taylor and how she felt in his arms.

But he couldn't ignore his responsibilities. Never had. Not since he'd been ten years old and those who should have known better disregarded theirs. In the blink of an eye, Taylor had become his responsibility.

By the time he parked the Mustang behind the bar, the crowd had diminished, though escape proved impossible.

"Hey, Cade, get lucky?"

"Nah, she looks too sweet for our man."

Cade frowned at the snide innuendoes, and his hands balled into fists at his sides. As he crossed the bar, he felt his sister's gaze follow him, but he refused to acknowledge her silent questioning and gave a dismissive wave to the rest. He eyeballed the bar. He needed a drink. And time to think.

Filling a glass with the remains of half-melted ice from the ice bucket, he poured himself a whiskey and headed straight for the back room.

Perfume. Taylor's perfume. Cade skidded to a halt. The tantalizing fragrance of roses and lilacs assailed his senses the moment he walked in. His eyes shuttered and he inhaled, remembering how her skin had smelt too. Now he'd never be able to rid her from his mind, or body.

Sinking into the chair behind his desk, he held his glass. The ice clinked and swirled a watery path through the golden liquid. He mentally counted to ten and waited.

The door banged open, and he glanced at his watch. "Dead on time."

"You and I need to talk, Cade."

He gave a resigned sigh. "Why am I not surprised it's you, Katie?"

"Now don't get all uppity with me."

"As if I would." He raised his hands in surrender as his sister stepped into the room and closed the door behind her.

"The bar is closing. I've cashed up."

"Thanks." But Cade knew there was more to come.

"So, who is she?"

"None of your business," he said quietly.

"Sure it is. I've got to look after my brother. Your history goes before you."

"What history?" He tried to deny it, but knew his track record with women was about to play against him.

"That's exactly what I mean. Too many to remember. The female species drop at your feet like flies."

"And your point is?" Cade tempered his tone. He put up with Katie's nosiness because he loved her. Unfortunately, she didn't take the hint.

"The point is they drool over you, and you play the game, one after another. This one's different."

"How so?" He narrowed his gaze on Katie, surprised by her intuitiveness. But she didn't give up. She was on a roll.

"Well, for a start, she's got clothes on."

So far. Cade's mind whirred.

"She's a wedding planner," he offered by way of an appeasement. Seeing the surprise on his sister's face, he nearly laughed out loud, despite himself.

Katie's eyes twinkled. "Anything I should know about?"

"Nope."

"Oh, yeah, that's right. I forgot you're commitment shy."

"Got that in one."

"You can't keep blaming them, Cade."

His jaw tightened along with every muscle in his body, unwanted memories taking him instantly to a sad, dark place he didn't want to visit. It always did at the mention of his parents. "That's none of your business. You were too young to know what went on."

"Perhaps, but I've seen the consequences."

And *he'd* lived them. "Forget it. It's not up for discussion."

"So?" Her foot tapped a tattoo as she stood with her hands on her hips. "I'm waiting."

"You're not giving up, are you?"

She gave him a quirky "I told you so" smile.

"Stubborn as a mule."

"We're from the same gene pool, Cade, so don't forget to look at yourself."

Cade exhaled. His sister's determined look spoke volumes. "Taylor's...a business associate," he said. "She's going to help me promote the new cocktail bar."

"Her! She doesn't look the bar type. What's in it for her, besides a big consulting fee?"

"There doesn't have to be."

"I know you, don't forget," Katie said, waggling her finger at him.

Ten long minutes later, Katie thankfully gave in and left him, though peace didn't come. He warred internally. Intuition told him to run a mile. Yet, instinctively, he knew he wouldn't walk away from Taylor. She needed him.

She needs to lose her virginity. I can help in that department.

Eyes squeezed shut, Cade tried to block Taylor from his mind and his body. Everything hummed with a heat so damned urgent it took all the willpower in the world to hold back. He wanted to jump into bed with her right now. To make love, long and slow and sweet, then hot and fast, over and over until he could erase his need for her.

Why so fierce? Why so urgent?

Hell if he knew. He wasn't some pubescent school kid needing to get his rocks off. Yet the thought of Taylor with another guy gnawed a path straight to his gut.

Damn it, he didn't want to care, but he did. And that spelled danger, big time.

Chapter Three

Nita sidelined Taylor the moment she walked into her office the next morning. "Looks like you had a long night."

"Forget it." Taylor held up her hand. "You can stop hinting right there. Nothing happened."

"You mean you...didn't?"

Taylor fixed her attention on her diary in front of her, but with Nita hovering, she knew she had no chance of evasion. "No," she finally answered with a shake of her head, "we didn't. In fact, Cade Harper was the perfect gentleman."

Nita dropped the morning mail in front of her. "Darn. You don't want a gentleman. You want fantasy."

And therein lay the problem. Taylor had fantasies and dreams all night. Hours and hours of vivid imagery, a heat coiled way down low, when she believed she could feel Cade's touch, needy and urgent. It had been a long and lonely night.

"Right, let's get down to business," she said, trying to hide her mood. She dropped her briefcase beside her desk and switched on her computer.

And what about your dreams?

The question he'd asked her last night replayed—again.

She had dreamed—a long time ago. But Taylor had learnt reality and dreams didn't mix. Death had come along, and she'd been given a sad reprieve wrapped in a shroud of guilt, and with it, the chance to dream had been stolen—until now.

Now she dreamed of something quite different.

Sex with Cade. Wonderfully hot sex.

Taylor squeezed her eyes shut. Oh, Lord, she was a wreck.

Morning passed in a whirl of messages and creating paper plans for seating arrangements for an upcoming wedding. It was also tied up with tangled dreams about Cade Harper and, by the afternoon, unable to concentrate, she found herself glancing at the phone every few minutes. Her hands shook as she picked up her cup and sipped her mochaccino.

"Here are the monthly accounts." Nita placed them in front of her. "Still no call?"

"No." Taylor refused to look Nita in the eye. "All afternoon I've played the will he, won't he game, just like when we were kids, picking the petals off a daisy. He loves me, he loves me not..." Her voice trailed off.

"This isn't about love."

"I know. It's about straight sex."

"Well, not necessarily," Nita countered, giving Taylor a knowing wink. "Taylor, you work too much. You need to get out, get a life."

"I have a life." Taylor picked up the accounts. The absolute last thing she wanted to focus on right now.

"No you don't."

"This is my life, Nita."

"Yes, but sometimes we need a shake-up."

"I don't think I'm up to another shake-up," she admitted.

"I never thought you'd give up."

Her denial came automatically. "I'm not giving up."

"Really? So why haven't you phoned him?"

Yeah, why?

Because she was scared witless and had got herself in too deep. The way Cade made her feel with just one kiss scared her.

"It's a stupid idea, he's..."

"Everything you've ever wanted."

"I don't *want him.*"

"Liar," Nita countered, laughing. "Maybe not, but you *really* need him. You made a mistake with Rob."

"Leave him out of it." Taylor dropped the folder of accounts back onto her desk.

"Why? It all boils down to Rob, doesn't it? You mistook liking and tenderness for love. You thought you'd fallen in love with the boy next door. That's all."

But there was more to it. Deep stuff. Emotions Taylor didn't know how to deal with. Or if she wanted to.

Her shoulders sagged, and she slumped back in her seat. "Okay, I agree, Cade is one hunky guy. He oozes charm and sex appeal and has a body to die for."

"Are you listening to yourself? You're bonkers about the guy."

"Am not."

Nita rubbed her hands together with blatant glee. "Oh, Taylor, I can read you like a book. Time to move on and test the waters again."

Nita was right—sort of. But in truth, Taylor knew she was different from her family. They married their first loves, were hyper-achievers with mega brains. Her parents were mathematicians, her brother a scientist and her sister a doctor—while she had become a wedding planner. Talk about a square peg in a round hole. And a disappointment.

He's the One

As the clock edged past four, Taylor found herself staring into nothing, lost in a world of "what ifs". The peal of the phone dragged her from her reverie. Scooping up the handheld, she punched the talk button.

"Creative Weddings."

"Taylor?"

Her mouth opened. It shut. It opened again.

"You there?"

Suddenly, her belly did flip-flops and her breasts felt heavy with need. "Um, yes."

"It's Cade Harper."

Oh, yeah. She knew that.

"I would've called earlier, but I had a problem at the bar."

Think of something, anything. "Can I help?"

Cade chuckled, a heavy velvet sound that rumbled from deep down in his chest. She'd heard it yesterday, felt it beneath her fingertips when they'd kissed. Oh, Lord.

"You're the problem."

Her heartbeat stilled, and the flip-flops in her belly skidded to a halt. "I see."

"I've been trying to arrange extra staff for tonight."

"Tonight?"

"You still want to go out, don't you?"

"Out?" *He means a date, stupid—a D-A-T-E.*

Another of Cade's deep laughs echoed down the phone line and sent a river of shivery tingles up and down her spine.

"You're repeating everything I say. I thought you were a lady of more words than that."

Get it together, Sullivan.

"Mind you, those little breathless sighs of yours sure do put a guy in the mood."

Taylor clamped her lips together. She couldn't believe it. "You phoned."

"I said I would. You didn't believe me?" Suddenly, the timbre of Cade's voice changed, the light, teasing tone replaced by a seriousness she hadn't heard before. "When I give my word, Taylor, I mean it. I stick to it."

"And you said we'd get to know one another."

"That's why I rang."

Oh, dear Lord.

"How about tonight?"

"Tonight," she squeaked. Tonight seemed too soon. "Know as in the biblical sense?"

"We gotta walk before we run. I'll pick you up at seven-thirty, okay?"

She nodded, then realized she needed to speak. "Fine." Though she couldn't help but wonder what "walking" involved. The phone clicked, and Taylor hit the off button and dropped it into its cradle. For several minutes, she simply sat, stunned.

The roller coaster ride had begun.

She glanced at her watch. Four-thirty.

She had a date with Cade.

After grabbing her bag, she dug deep for her keys.

Nita walked into the office as Taylor slipped her bag over her shoulder. "Going somewhere?"

"On a date." She gave her assistant the thumbs up.

"Way to go. Don't forget the condoms."

Oh, boy.

For three long, scary hours, Taylor paced her bedroom. She wished for the hundredth time she'd never come up with such a harebrained scheme. Besides, what the hell did a woman wear to entice a man? Taylor surveyed the heap of clothes on her bed. It had been so long; she didn't have clue. In fact, she'd never really dated. Rob had always just been there. They'd started kindergarten together, gone through primary and high school. Everyone thought of them as a couple. Always.

But *always* didn't work out.

Taylor eyed a gray dress and jacket, fingered the fine-textured fabric while a bubble of hysteria forced her closer to turning tail and running like crazy.

"Typical. A wardrobe full of clothes and nothing to wear. Nothing remotely sexy." Taylor sank down on the bed and hugged the gray suit to her chest. "Boring. That's what it says. Boring, boring. All you've got is work, no life."

But how could she forge a life when others set the benchmark? Her family "put up" with her creative side, believed she'd see the light and one day go to university—and be just like them.

But they were wrong. She could never be like them.

As the iridescent green numbers of the radio clock on her bedside table ticked ever closer to seven-thirty, Taylor eyed herself in the full-length mirror, saw the fear and the flush of panic coloring cheeks. She snatched up the closest dress, a sleek black sheath with cutaway shoulders, and slipped it on, twirling in front of the mirror. She caught her reflection again.

"Tonight's the night," she whispered, and traced her lips with her fingertips.

Her eyes fluttered closed. She could feel Cade, his lips on hers. So beautiful. Heat pooled in her belly, and she dropped her hand there, sliding a soft caress over her stomach.

A knock hammered home on her front door, and her head snapped up.

Damn. With clothes scattered about, the room certainly didn't resemble a passion pit. Taylor corralled her scattered clothes and shoved them into the wardrobe. She grabbed her jacket and purse and slipped her feet into a pair of strappy black sandals and made a beeline for the door.

Taylor swore her heart stopped as she opened the door to Cade and had to force herself to breathe. Difficult when he simply took her breath away.

Dressed in dark trousers and shirt that set off his outdoorsy tan, Cade stood under the nightlight on her doorstep, a sports jacket slung over one shoulder.

He looked so *very* good, and Taylor had to force herself not to reach out and touch him, run her fingers through his hair.

Dark eyes shrouded by long, thick lashes held her captive, and his smile deepened his dimples. She wanted to kiss them.

Finally, she managed to speak. "You're on time."

"You didn't think I would be?"

"I thought perhaps the bar might keep you busy."

"You don't quite believe me yet, do you, Taylor?"

Heat scalded her cheeks. Guilty as charged. She chose immediate retreat. "I'll just get my jacket."

"What? Not going to invite me in?" he teased.

Taylor didn't know what to say, and deep down wasn't even sure what she should say, or what was expected. Instead, she shook her head and, with her jacket and bag in one hand, she flicked the lock on the front door and pulled it closed.

Feathery fronds of lavender guarded either side of the path and tinged the night air as she walked with Cade toward the car. At the white picket gate, he halted and turned to her with a serious expression. He leant close.

Hope and expectation fired inside Taylor. Her lips parted, a shivery heat coloring her world. Was Cade going to kiss her?

"You may have put the ultimate proposal to me, Taylor, but don't fret, I won't rush you. I'm no uncouth youth who can't wait to get going. I *can*," he said with determination.

Taylor swallowed hard and squashed her disappointment.

The thing was, could she?

Parked at the curb was the Mustang, all curves and angles and rich, real leather. It looked like a *real* car.

Taylor slid in. "Where are we going?"

Cade caught her tension as he eased the car into the evening traffic. Funny, he felt the same. Excited. Adrenaline pumping. He struggled to find his voice. "Hope you like seafood."

"Yes." Her reply was quiet, almost ethereal, and it turned him on without even trying. She looked away.

Cade changed gears. He wound the window down and then back up. He glanced over at her. All stiff and rigid, hands folded tightly in her lap. He smiled. "I feel like kid again," he said. "I don't know what to say."

"Well, if it's any consolation, I'm nervous too."

"Yeah, I guess you would be." The anticipation of finding out more about Taylor and why she'd waited so long stirred his imagination, and more.

Dressed in a black dress that skimmed her curves, she reminded him of his cars. Taylor had curves he'd love to caress.

"We can start easy," he said and reached over and took her hand in his. He heard her exhale, accompanied by a tiny shudder.

He wasn't doing any better. His groin had taken a direct

hit. He tried to think of anything except sex.

He flicked another glance at Taylor. So beautiful, with her hair in a sleek chignon, exposing her neck and those sexy earrings that dangled from impossibly seductive earlobes. Oh, man. He had it bad. Sex with Taylor was definitely on his mind.

"Do you know I sat up all night because of you, wondering what lay beneath that uptight exterior you portray?"

"There's nothing beneath…"

"Really?" he interrupted. "Nothing, as in naked?" His eyes twinkled.

"No!" Taylor's denial rent the confines of the car. "I am who I am," she said. Her smile slipped, and she went to pull her hand from his.

"Oh, no, you don't. That stays here. Foreplay, remember? Though I must admit, the possibility of you naked beneath that sleek black dress is going to send me over the edge. My concentration has taken a nose dive."

"Keep your eyes on the road, Cade."

"Yes, ma'am."

How the hell would he survive the evening, and how could he react so strongly to a woman he'd only just met? But he did, and nothing had prepared him for the jolt of heat pinning him to the spot the moment Taylor had opened the door. From that moment, he'd been on the verge of losing it.

And right now, he definitely wanted to lose his hands in her hair, unpin it as he'd done last night, let it slide over his hands, feel her lips beneath his.

He wanted to explore, not listen to his conscience.

She hadn't taken her hand away, though, and that strengthened his hope. He traced a pattern across her palm, enjoying the feel of her skin beneath his.

"Late into the night, my mind played tricks on me. Had me guessing. Want to know what I came up with?" he asked. He saw her hesitate and continued. "I reckon you're frightened of life."

"That's ridiculous. I run a successful business."

"I did a bit of research."

Taylor's jaw dropped, and this time she yanked hard and managed to pull her hand away. "You checked up on me?"

"Sure thing. Just as you did on me."

Cade drove the Mustang toward the Harbor Bridge, which spanned from the North Shore to the central city, where the city's fathers had reclaimed land at the waterfront over a hundred years earlier.

"How long have you been interested in classic cars?"

Taylor's unexpected question caught him off guard. "Good change of topic," he teased. A tiny smile played on his mouth, but he kept his eyes on the road. It didn't prevent him from reaching for her hand again, though.

This time, Taylor didn't resist.

"As a kid, I used to hang out at the speedway," he said as they passed the container wharves. "My passion is anything fast. When I started making some serious money, I bought an old car and renovated it in my spare time."

"This one?"

"Yep," he said with pride. "This is the baby of the group."

"There's more than one?"

"Four to be exact."

"Impressive."

"I'll show you them sometime."

A flutter of laughter escaped her lips. "That sounds like

your version of etchings."

Cade wriggled his brows suggestively. "Why don't you come up and see me sometime," he said in a fake accent.

"I don't think you're quite right. Wasn't it Mae West who said that?"

"Oops." He laughed with her, and he began circling her palm with his thumb.

Foreplay. Verbal foreplay.

It had started. "But if you'd like to see the cars, I'm happy to show you."

"Thank you. I'd like that. This car is certainly exotic. It must take a long time to restore them."

"Yeah."

"Dedication and commitment."

"That's about it."

"Yet you're anti-commitment."

"If you mean marriage, then you're dead right on that score," he agreed. The change in his tone had been slight, but definite.

"Do you drive them all?"

"Of course. Cars are for driving, not simply for show. They're machines, just like humans, and meant to be used."

Taylor remembered the way Cade had caressed the car's curves, almost tenderly, blessing its beauty. Would he be as gentle with her? What would his touch *really* be like?

"We're here," he announced as they pulled into a car park along the waterfront.

Taylor glanced up at the two-story building nestled into the curve at Okahu Bay, one of the city's now-exclusive neighborhoods. In previous years, the building had been part of the city's control center for wastewater, and more recently had been converted into a top restaurant.

Cade switched off the engine and everything went quiet. The butterflies in Taylor's stomach performed somersaults.

He shifted to face her. "There's something I've wanted to do since last night." Cade's mouth covered hers. Gone was the tentative and gentle kiss. This was hot and demanding—breathless. Beautiful.

He pulled back, eyes darkened and lids hooded. Bedroom eyes, she thought. He smiled at her with a lopsided grin that tugged at her heart. "I couldn't wait."

She wanted his kiss too. A little part had wanted it to go on forever. But then a sad and insidious guilt snaked through her, breaking her soul.

Remember, this is an experiment. To be experienced only once.

A harsh cry wrenched from her lips. "No." She wiped the back of her hand across her mouth, trying to erase temptation. She caught Cade's accusing gaze, felt it rest on her mouth, and her hand fell away. "I'm sorry. You took me unawares," she said, feeling like the prim woman he thought her.

"How old are you, Taylor?"

"Twenty-four."

"That's what I don't understand. You're very successful, run a thriving business, but in this day and age, most women of your age aren't—"

"Virgins," she finished for him.

"Yeah."

"Well, that's tough," she bit back. "Because I am. It's not a disease."

"I never said that."

"No, you didn't. I know I'm the odd one out. I have been all my life. Nothing new there."

Needing to put space between her and Cade, Taylor climbed out of the car into the chilly night. Goose bumps sprinted down her bare arms, and her breath misted into the darkness.

He came to stand beside her. "I'm sorry. I didn't mean to touch a sore subject."

"Don't worry. It's nothing." But it wasn't. It was her past and her present, something that never went away and with which she lived daily.

"Come on." Cade turned her toward the restaurant. "Dinner awaits. Let's put all this morose talk behind us for the night and enjoy ourselves." He held out his hand to her.

She hesitated for a fraction, then took it and gave him a fleeting smile. "Why not? We only live once," she said.

Rob had lived only once, leaving guilt and sadness behind. Her guilt—that she'd lied to him. But how could she have told a dying man she no longer loved him?

Sedate and sophisticated, Hammerheads oozed exclusivity and enjoyed the reputation of being the best seafood restaurant in town. With its arched Palladian windows opened to a panoramic view of the harbor and the myriad of boats moored alongside, it set an exquisite scene for diners.

Approached immediately by the maitre d', Cade guided Taylor across the restaurant, his hand resting on the small of her back. His touch shattered her concentration, and she struggled to focus on anything except the handsome man at her side.

Once they were seated, the waiter provided menus and a wine list. Cade discussed various wines with him, surprising her. It must have showed as he lowered the wine list and gave a curt nod to the waiter, who slipped away.

"I'm not just a backyard bar boy."

"I realize that."

His steady gaze held hers. "Do you?"

"Yes. Of course."

"You're not really sure about me, admit it. I said I wondered who the real Taylor Sullivan was. Now I get it."

"Get what?" Taylor sipped at her iced water.

"You're stuck in a void. A prim little world that you can't see out of. You said you were the square peg. Well, that's just it. You pigeonhole people too."

"I do not. That's my..." Taylor slammed her lips together. That was her family. Not her. Surely?

"Yes, you do. You think because someone comes from the wrong side of the tracks he can't be..." Cade's gaze skimmed the room and back to her. "Can't be cultured," he finally said with a sneer.

"That's not true. You're making me sound like a snob."

He shrugged and reached for his glass, then swallowed its contents in one long gulp.

Taylor couldn't take her eyes off his throat. Long. Strong. The movement as he swallowed.

Heat washed over her, and beneath the table her toes curled in her sandals. Finally, she found her tongue. "I'm sorry, Cade. I didn't mean to insult you. I...I'm not a snob. In fact, if there's anyone out of their depth right now, that'd be me," she said honestly.

Cade might make her feel unsure, but her own emotions had set her world all topsy-turvy. She needed to get back in control—fast.

Taylor cast her gaze about the room and choked back a sadness. Lovers. Couples. Everyone a duo. Soft touches, a caress here, a secretive smile there. Would tonight be her time to enjoy romance, even for one night? Just the thought of it set her heart rate into overdrive, and she fidgeted with her water glass. She racked her brain for non-contentious conversation.

"How did you know Hugh Prendergast and Brianna Bennett?" she finally asked.

Cade lowered his glass and eased back into the luxurious leather chair. He rested a hand on the pure white linen tablecloth, and Taylor found herself fixated for a moment on his fingers.

"I grew up with Hugh, me on the wrong side of the tracks, him definitely on the other. Schools are zoned and our suburb bordered on his, so we ended up at the same junior school, then high school. Hugh was the nerd. Everyone took the Mickey out of him. It wasn't nice."

"Bullies are never nice."

"No." Cade's tone hardened. "I sort of took him under my wing, and we discovered a love of making things."

"What sort of things?"

"Small inventions, electronic gadgets." He twirled his wineglass and took a sip. Taylor watched as his tongue wiped across his top lip and found herself doing the same. She couldn't breathe and tried to swallow. Nothing worked. Was it hot in here or what?

"That'd explain how Hugh became one of the big players in electronics," she reasoned. The waiter arrived at that moment, ready to take their order, and Taylor sensed Cade's relief at the interruption. She eyed the vast menu, unsure she had the mental dexterity to choose anything.

Except another kiss.

"How about the seared game fish," Cade suggested. "It's delicious."

She lowered the menu. "You've been here before?"

Cade gave their orders to the waiter before answering. "Several times." The twinkle in his bedroom eyes offered a silent challenge.

Taylor's throat thickened. "With other women?"

"Of course."

"You go out with a lot of women." It wasn't a question, but a statement, one to which she already knew the answer.

"And that makes you feel comfortable or uncomfortable?"

Taylor reached for her napkin, playing for time. Foreplay, he'd said. *Fun.* She slid the napkin from the silver holder and unfurled the crisp white linen, laid it on her lap, then looked directly at him. "Oh, definitely comfortable," she said, smiling, knowing he'd turned her statement back on her.

His grin widened, and he folded his arms across his chest. Her mouth dry, she reached for her glass and took a steadying sip of wine. Her gaze never left his.

"How so?"

Oh, boy. Things were heating up. She'd been hooked, and now he reeled her in. "It means you're...um, experienced," she finally admitted.

"And you get a good teacher."

Her jaw dropped, and he gave her a cheesy grin, as if very pleased with himself.

"Never believe what the gossips tell you, Taylor. I know I have a profile in the papers. Owning a string of successful businesses ensures that."

"You don't mind?"

"Why would I? It doesn't do any harm to my business."

"And that's important?"

"Of course it is. Isn't it to you?"

"Well, yes," she agreed.

Cade eyed her above the rim of his crystal glass. "I'm not a monk. I know a lot of women and go out with some, and to bed sometimes too."

Blood boiled in Taylor's veins, along with something else…something indefinable. It wasn't a nice feeling. She leveled her gaze with his. "So that makes you perfect."

"You think I'm perfect?"

"Oh, now you're putting words in my mouth."

Cade suggested they wait before ordering dessert. "How about we take a stroll outside?"

Taylor eyed the deck attached to the restaurant.

Dare she? With the other diners around, she felt safe—safe from her own actions. But outside, with only the stars and the caw of the occasional gull, she would be alone with Cade.

"You too scared to be alone with me?" he challenged, surprising her as if he could read her mind.

"Of course not."

"Liar." And he held out his hand.

Taylor dropped her napkin to the table and pushed back her chair. If she wasn't scared, then why were her legs already like jelly? She took Cade's hand, but once outside, a shiver slid up and down her spine.

"Cold?" Cade asked.

She shook her head, but he pulled her into his embrace

and wrapped an arm around her shoulders. The shivers continued, though Taylor knew it had nothing to do with the climate. She inhaled his scent. Masculine. Sexy. Tempting.

The moon hung high in the night sky, surrounded by an array of stars and the inky blackness of the ocean. The soft slap of waves rolling in with the tide brought the tangy fragrance of sea spray.

"See that cluster of stars?" Cade pointed skyward. "That's the Southern Cross." He leant toward her, his breath a warm flutter across her cheek. "Crux lies along the Milky Way, surrounded by Centaurus, and at the foot of the cross," he said, indicating the stars which made up the constellation, "is Acrux. It's the brightest star."

"Very impressive."

"A tick in my favor. That's good." He returned her smile.

With his back to the view, Cade leant against the railing and pulled her to rest between his parted thighs. Her belly did a double flip, aware the instant his very blatant arousal pulsed against her.

"When did you learn all this?" she asked, trying to stall the urge to cling to him and not let go.

"When I was a kid." But his smile disappeared, and his eyes dulled. "Too many hours spent stargazing when my parents couldn't stand each other. Easier to bury my head in books and the universe than listen to the bickering."

"Arguments?"

"You could say that," he answered. "See that one?" he said, bringing her with him. He wrapped his free arm around her waist, fingers caressing her stomach through her dress.

A fluttering sigh escaped Taylor's parted lips. The night air may have cooled her skin, but her body had definitely started a slow burn.

"That one is Virgo. It's only visible through April to July and is known as the Maiden. It represents almost every famous and powerful female in mythology."

"I rather like that. Being aligned with powerful women."

"Women are always powerful. They just don't know it," Cade murmured cryptically against her ear.

But the moment of seclusion didn't last as the doors from the restaurant to the deck opened and a family group bundled out into the cooling night.

Cade didn't say anything, but gave her a quick kiss on her lips, so soft Taylor wasn't sure it even happened. Except that her mouth tingled. He guided her back into the restaurant, and they retook their seats.

Dessert had been served.

"This is delicious." Taylor gloried in the velvet smooth ambrosia as it slid over her tongue. She looked up at Cade. "You want to try?"

"Sure."

A slow secretive smile curled the corners of Taylor's mouth. She might have been a wreck earlier, scouring her wardrobe for something sexy to wear, but as she offered Cade her spoon, sex was definitely on her mind.

He wrapped his fingers around hers, and his lips parted. Taylor's breathing quickened. She imagined him kissing her, his tongue sliding over her skin.

He licked the spoon, dark eyes fueled with desire, holding hers.

"Taste is everything." He wiped the tip of his tongue across his top lip. The timbre of his voice had changed, charged now.

Beneath the table, she squeezed her thighs together.

"Do you say that to all your women?" She heard her voice.

She sounded sultry, even sexy. Boy, was she on a roll. This was easy. She smiled to herself. Who would have thought Taylor Sullivan could be sexy, smart, heck, even sassy?

"Are we back to that again?"

Taylor shook her head, struggling to concentrate, able to focus only on what Cade did with that yummy mouth of his. She breathed slowly, until she finally found control, or at least a semblance of it. "Just wondering if it was one of your moves. One you've practiced, you know, to get your dates in the mood."

Cade's smile dipped slightly, and his dimples tempted her again. "Ah...that mood. Hmm, let me see. A fine restaurant, great meal, wine, good conversation." He took a slow sip of his wine, his gaze never once leaving her face. "Does that equal sex for dessert?"

Did it? Taylor leant forward on her seat.

"I know this is your game, Taylor, but how about allowing me take the lead, sometime, hmm? Wouldn't want to spoil the surprise, now, would we?"

"Spoilsport."

He laughed, tossed his napkin aside, pushed his chair back and stood. "Absolutely. Come on, I think it's time we got out of here."

"Funny how the distance traveled on the outward journey always seems less than the return, isn't it?" Cade said as they reached the highest span of the bridge.

Taylor, however, simply offered him a slight smile. A sweet smile, and his nether regions reacted.

His attraction to her was in no doubt. Long-term or commitment, however, was definitely not on the agenda. Both had stated that fact.

Cade exhaled a long, drawn-out breath. What was it about Taylor that had him agreeing to her blatantly tempting proposal? He gave her a sideways glance. She'd been quiet for a while, lost in her own thoughts, just as he was.

Taylor Sullivan. Businesswoman. Beautiful. Sexy. His gaze lowered to her ankles. They were crossed, a very demure action, but her shoes with their wafer-thin heels were nothing like demure.

His blood pumped faster. Yep. Definitely a recipe for pleasure.

As they neared the off ramp to the northern beaches, Taylor's phone buzzed. She gave him a quick "I'm sorry" and reached for it.

"Babette, what's the problem?"

"Babette?" Cade mouthed.

Taylor wagged her finger at him, and he clamped down on his laughter.

"He wants what?" Color flamed Taylor's cheeks, and from her reaction, Cade knew this was one of *those* calls.

"What does she want to know? Come on, tell me." He couldn't stem his smile or the chuckle deep down in his belly. This was his moment to help. "Shoot, Taylor."

Taylor covered the mouthpiece, and her face took on a strained expression. "Babette wants to know about multiple orgasms."

Chapter Four

"So he says I should be able to, you know...at least three times a night."

"Oh." Taylor's gut churned. How the heck did she answer that?

Cade's brows wriggled suggestively. She didn't know where to look. Not at Cade, that was for sure. Looking at him made her wonder what she was missing and fired up her fantasies.

"So what do I tell him? I mean, I love him, but, heavens, I don't want to be charted on my success rate."

"And you shouldn't be," Taylor affirmed, battling to get her brain cells back on track and focus on her client's problem, not on the man who sat far too close to her.

What was it about pheromones?

Right now she reckoned she was overdosing on them.

She racked her brain in the hope she could come up with something witty, something real to answer Babette's dilemma.

"What do I do, Taylor? How many do you have?"

"How many?" Taylor repeated, her throat closing up.

Cade's brows rose a fraction higher. Taylor turned away from his curiosity. Oh, dear Lord, could the man read her mind?

"Yeah, you know. Orgasms."

Her mouth opened and closed several times. She couldn't find her voice. Didn't have an answer, either.

"Well, it depends, I mean...hey, what..."

Cade yanked the phone from her grip. "Hi there, it's Cade Harper, Taylor's..." He hesitated, and his gaze slid in her direction briefly. "I'm her boyfriend."

"Since when?" Taylor elbowed him and tried to get the phone back, but he outmaneuvered her and drew the car quickly to a halt at the side of the road.

"This is an important client," she whispered urgently.

He covered the mouthpiece. "Then let me help. You want answers, don't you?"

"From you?"

"Why not? I've got plenty of experience. You said so yourself."

A groan slipped from Taylor's lips, and she sank back against her seat. She squeezed her eyes shut.

Perhaps she could click her heels and fly to Oz?

"Now, look, honey." Cade's voice purred down the phone line.

Taylor's eyes flicked open.

"Honey?" she mouthed, rolling her eyes at him, annoyed that the man sounded so calm and collected, not even a tad ruffled by Babette's direct questioning.

And damn it, the more honeyed he sounded, the more she bristled.

"You tell that man of yours it's his job to pleasure you, take you to heights you've never reached before," he said, gaze never once leaving Taylor's face.

Taylor couldn't believe what she was hearing. She went to speak, but he held up a hand, silencing her protests. And then he smiled, and she shut right up. Just like he wanted.

"Get him to try that spot. Yeah, that's the one. Get some books."

"Books!" Taylor almost screeched.

"Play a little. Experiment."

Her eyes nearly popped out of her head, and the frantic race of her pulse headed toward the boiling point. "Oh, my God. That client is down the drain." She groaned.

Cade chuckled, obviously in response to something witty from Babette. Taylor wished she could hear what was being said.

"Sure, she appreciates me," he answered. Cade reached for her hand, linking his fingers with hers and holding on tight, his humor-filled gaze resting on her. "I'm just what she ordered."

Taylor wished the moment would disappear.

"Okay, Babette, honey, you get that man organized. Tell him what *you* want." Cade clicked the phone off.

Silence echoed, but for only a heartbeat before Taylor rounded on Cade.

"Babette, honey! Oh, puh-lease. That is so O.T.T. With that line, you qualify for Car Salesman of the Year."

Cade gave her one of his lopsided boyish grins. He shrugged. "She didn't seem to mind. And besides, I thought you would be pleased."

Taylor fought an internal battle. One part of her agreed with him—she should be relieved she didn't have to answer Babette—while the other part of her, heck more like ninety-percent, railed at her own inadequacies.

She should have been able to answer.

She shouldn't be so naïve.

She was embarrassed at her own ineptitude.

But there was no way she was going to let Cade see that. "Why should I be grateful to you?"

"Because I alleviated your client's worries. Good for any business, surely?"

"Alleviate? You practically told the woman to go buy every sex book in the city."

"Did not." Cade started up the car again.

"Oh, yes, you did—well, sort of. Experiment, then."

"Good for keeping the bedroom interesting."

Suddenly, Taylor wasn't too comfortable about where this discussion was heading.

To the bedroom, where else? And you've walked right into it.

"I see."

"You will, Taylor. You will."

Taylor stared into the passing darkness. She was drowning. Where was that damn life jacket again?

"Would you like to come in?" Taylor asked as Cade silenced the engine outside her house. He heard the soft, breathless lilt to her voice, heard her uncertainty.

"It's late," he answered, giving her a reprieve, but realizing in the same instant he really, really didn't want to.

"Oh." She sounded disappointed.

Good tactic—leave her wanting more. "It's not that I don't want to." Man, he had a hard-on and battled to stay focused, to... What was it he wanted to say?

"No, it's okay, I understand. It was a nice meal."

Cade stared down at Taylor, wondering what she was thinking. Her eyes had shuttered slightly, closing him out. But then, he didn't understand any of this himself. He cursed under his breath and dragged a hand through his hair. Placing his hands on her shoulders, he turned her toward him. He felt her silky skin beneath his fingertips, wanted to brush his hands along it. Instead, he bit back his rock-hard need. "Taylor, look at me."

She lifted her wide blue eyes to him.

A man could drown in those blue pools, he thought. Hell, he had. He choked back an oath. "This is awkward. One part of me wants to rush you right into bed and bury myself deep inside you, find out what's behind that veneer you present."

"I..."

He put a finger to her parted lips and felt her warm breath rush over his fingertip.

Stupid move. His need intensified.

"Shush. Unfortunately, the sensible part of me says hold on, take it easy, and the trouble is, I'm listening."

He walked her to the door, neither of them saying anything. Outside, the automatic security light switched on, and Cade felt like they were visible for the world to see. As Taylor fumbled with the lock, he reached across then took the key from her and opened the door. She turned to him, expectancy written on her beautiful face.

"Thank you for a lovely evening," she said, a sweet, tentative smile curving her delicious mouth.

"Well...um...yeah. It was good." Cade stumbled over his words—words he really meant, though in truth he felt like a pubescent school kid. Hell, he'd never *felt* so damned tongue tied before. He shoved his hands in his pockets. Not a good idea. It only drew the fabric over his very aroused status even more. "I've gotta go. I'll...um, see you."

Taylor didn't answer him, but walked inside and shut the

door behind her, leaving him with his conscience and his arousal, fighting for control.

Cade blew out a long, slow stream of air till there was nothing left. Why did he feel so let down? Damn it.

Because you wanted her, and you know she wanted you.

"So?" Nita asked Taylor the moment she walked in, dumping her bag and shucking out of her coat as she made a determined beeline toward her.

"Here comes trouble." Taylor tried to ignore Nita's early morning excitement and carried on sorting through the list of calls she had to make that morning for the Hayes wedding. The bride wanted Cinderella; the groom wanted medieval. Taylor only hoped she could fulfill their dreams with style.

Nita propped herself on the side of Taylor's desk. "I'm dying to know. Was he as good as expected?" She slapped her forehead. "Dumb question. Of course he was. I can see it written all over your face."

"Wishful imagination," Taylor shot back. "Besides, I'm not sure what you think you can see."

"Satisfaction guaranteed."

The pen in Taylor's hand jerked across the page. "Blast. Do you have to be so..."

"Curious?" Nita offered.

"This isn't a locker room."

"Come on, you know I've a knack for getting the lowdown, so give."

A weary sigh escaped Taylor's lips. Weary because she desperately needed sleep. And that was all Cade Harper's fault. Again. He may have refused her bed last night, but he'd still kept her awake into the wee hours of the morning. Awake and aroused two nights in a row.

"Now, no more prevaricating, Taylor. Spill."

"Prevaricate. Big word this time of the morning."

Nita gave her a wicked grin. "But it fits the bill, right? Come on. I've been wondering all night."

"Then you'll be disappointed."

"*No*. Don't do that to me. I even stayed in last night and watched TV in case you called. Then I ended up eating a half a tub of hokey pokey ice cream."

Taylor tried not to smile and failed. "And you say I need a life."

"I was worried."

"About me?" Keep busy. Keep occupied. Maybe then Nita would give up the inquisition. Taylor turned the page to view her appointments. "Thanks for your concern," she said, hoping her assistant would drop the subject. "There's no need. It was a date. That's all."

"I know it's important to you."

"Was. Past tense."

"What? You're joking. How can you give up on him? He's..."

"Not interested, that's what."

"Oh, honey, you've got it *so* wrong. Cade is definitely interested."

"Then how come he hasn't...we haven't...well, you know..." Taylor's voice trailed off. What was wrong with her? She was discussing her sex life—correction—her lack of a sex life, with Nita. Her assistant was a good friend and a great employee, but still, this was way too personal.

Taylor snapped her schedule book closed. "Damn Cade. The one time I let my guard down. I thought I could do this, and he turns out to be the wrong guy."

"That's where you're wrong."

"You keep saying that, but where's the evidence?"

"He took you to dinner, didn't he?"

"Yes."

"Kissed you?"

"Uh-huh." Definitely.

"Good. You at least reached first base."

"You make it sound like a competition."

"Not quite, but it's like a game of baseball. First base, second, third, et cetera. Besides, a little competition never hurt anyone."

Taylor's eyes widened in horror. "How many bases are there, exactly?" Her fingers gripped her pen, twisting it. Anything to stop her hands from shaking.

Nita shrugged and gave her a sheepish grin. "A few."

Oh, God. "This is worse than I expected."

"Okay, okay. Keep your pants on." Nita giggled at her own joke. "Well, maybe not."

"Nita!"

"Firstly, there's kissing, lip-to-lip lock. You've done that, right?"

Taylor nodded as the kissing video switched to auto replay in her brain. Hotter than hot. Cade Harper was one good kisser.

"Then there's the tongue. Well, his tongue and yours, actually." Nita eyed her.

"Don't ask me."

"Honey, one look at you and I don't need to. Now, let's see. Third base is the touchy-feely stuff."

"No more." Taylor held up her hand. "That's it. Don't ask

me anymore. Don't even look at me. I'm not sure I can do this. I mean, I want to." Man, did she want to. Cade set her pulses racing, without a doubt. "He's turned me down twice."

"Two times, huh?"

"What do you mean, huh?"

"That's serious." Nita's smile faded.

Taylor found herself sitting on the edge of her seat. Sweat beaded between her breasts, and her throat felt suddenly desert-dry. "Bad serious?"

"Yep."

The pen skittered from her fingers and across the desk. She needed a drink. "How bad?"

"Let's look at it this way. Cade's no slouch in the lady department, right?"

Taylor nodded. Definitely temptation in one hunky package.

"So all we have to do is get him *into* you, proverbially speaking, that is."

"What do you mean, *we*?"

"Taylor, don't they say two heads are better than one?"

"Yeah." Trepidation mounted to dangerous proportions. "I'm not sure I like that look on your face, Nita. What have you got in mind?" She really shouldn't have asked, but couldn't help herself.

A devious glint darkened Nita's green eyes, and she gave Taylor a know-it-all sort of smile. "Wait and see. Like Cinderella, you'll get your man."

"But Cinders wanted the whole kit and caboodle. She wanted marriage to Prince Charming and the whole two-point-four kids. I *don't* want commitment, remember? I just want to get on with my life, get this whole thing over with."

"You need a plan. You phoned Cade yet?"

"No."

"What d'ya mean, no? How are you going to get that boy between the sheets unless you're in his face? Women are allowed to phone the male species, you know."

Desperation churned in Taylor's belly. "What do I say? 'So, Cade, when do we get between the sheets'?"

"Sounds proactive."

"Humbug," Taylor wailed. "What on earth am I doing?"

"Oh, Taylor, Taylor. Boy, do you need me."

"Like a hole in the head." Taylor hugged her planner to her chest as a protective shield, but as Nita chuckled, Taylor realized she had no way out. Nita was like a dog with a bone, and she wasn't about to let go.

"Come on. I'll get the coffee, then we can get down and strategize."

"You make it sound like an armored attack."

"Could be." She tapped the side of her nose as if she had some huge secret she was about to divulge. "A lady needs her armor."

"In that case, you'd better make my coffee strong and black."

"An espresso, coming right up. And while I'm doing that, take a look at some reading material." Nita dug into the leather tote and passed Taylor a pile of books.

Taylor skimmed over the titles. "Read..." Oh, Lordy.

Sex and the Single Man.

Want It Hot?

"You better make that a double shot espresso."

Chapter Five

"Man, are you grumpy." Zane Harper straddled the rickety wooden chair in front of Cade's desk.

Cade hissed out a resigned sigh. It didn't look as if his younger brother would move any time soon. What was it with the Harper clan that they thought they could stick their noses into his business?

"Back off, Zane." The warning issued as it was, his brother should have realized he was on dangerous ground. He didn't.

"Yep, definitely cantankerous. Katie said you weren't your usual chirpy self this morning."

Cade picked at a stray thread on his jeans. It started to unravel. Typical! "Get lost."

Zane folded his arms across the back of the chair. "Late night, was it?"

Cade grunted. "None of your damn business."

"Now that's where you're wrong. Trust me. You know I look up to you. You're my elder brother, after all."

"Try looking for the exit instead."

"Why would I do that when I can see you need to talk? Anything you want to tell me?"

"You're joking. You'd spread gossip around the bar in ten seconds flat."

Zane grinned. "There's gossip?"

Cade's mouth turned down and his hands fisted at his sides. He wanted to punch his brother's lights out. Frustration gnawed in his gut; hell, in his groin too, if he was truthful. He'd had a hard-on since...well, since Taylor Sullivan waltzed into his bar with a proposal that was as outlandish as it was exciting, to which, jerk that he was, he'd agreed.

Trouble was, belatedly, he'd come up with some fool idea of gentlemanly behavior.

Dumb move. All the cold showers in Antarctica wouldn't ease the ache he felt right now.

He looked up at his brother. "What are you looking so pleased about?"

"Just figured it out. You said you *didn't* have a late night."

Cade felt the pulse in his jaw flicker and gritted his teeth.

"You didn't get laid last night, is that it?"

"Don't be so crude."

"We're family. I'm looking out for you. Katie said some classy chick came in here the other night."

"I don't need looking after, Zane. I've looked after myself since I was ten years old, remember?"

"Yeah, and you haven't forgotten it. When are you going to let it go?"

"What is it with you and Katie? Both of you trying to psychoanalyze me or something?"

Zane simply smiled, which didn't help Cade's mood one iota.

"At the risk of repeating myself, *mate*, get lost."

Zane held up both hands in surrender. "Okay. I get the picture. You don't want to talk about her."

"Her?"

"The lady you've got the hots for."

"What makes you say that?"

A rumble of laughter rolled from Zane's chest. "Brother, I can read you like a book."

Just then the phone rang, and Cade sent a prayer up for its inventor. He picked up the handheld and eyed the display panel. He shot Zane a non-too-subtle hint to hit the road.

"Okay, I'm going." Zane winked, turned and exited, closing the door behind him. "It's her," Cade heard Zane call to the bar patrons.

Cade groaned aloud. He'd kill his brother with his bare hands.

He flicked the phone on, aware of the upped tempo of his heartbeat and the sudden sheen of perspiration on his brow. But that was nothing compared to the burning need in his pants.

"Hello, Taylor."

There was no sound at first except a soft feathering of her breath down the phone line.

"Taylor?"

"I...yes, it's me. I...um...want to thank you for dinner last night. It was very... enjoyable."

"Even though you didn't get what you wanted?" Not right away, he added silently.

"I thought I should see your new premises, get an idea of what you want."

You, sweetheart. Cade smiled. His brain warned him repeatedly to slow down and take it easy, not to scare her off, advice he was, by the second, struggling to listen to.

From his office, Cade could hear the cacophony of music

and laughter from customers on the other side of the door. It was late in the day, and already the bar hummed. It would be a good night for business, but definitely not a good night to bring Taylor here. He'd never hear the end of it.

"I'll be there in five."

"Now?"

Wired, Cade strode to the door, still holding the phone. "Sure. Isn't that what you want?"

"Yes." Taylor's reply was soft, and he barely heard it. But the fact that she hadn't hesitated brought a quick smile.

"Are you still at work?"

"Yes, I've got two weddings this weekend."

"More fools biting the dust," Cade muttered beneath his breath as he hung up.

The five minutes it took to drive to Taylor's seemed to take way too long. He came to a halt outside her tiny office located in the heart of Devonport's village and scooted up the path.

She opened the door wide and smiled, but he didn't move.

"Hello."

For some reason, Cade wanted to wait right there and remember the moment, take it all in.

Dressed in a matching camel-colored dress and jacket, she bespoke elegance, all woman. Cade wondered for the umpteenth time what she'd be like lying beneath him. Oh, boy, he had it bad. He expelled a long breath.

"So this is where all the action takes place?" he said as he moved about her showroom and office. Swathes of bridal silks and satins hung from one wall, photos of her clients decorated another, while shoes, headpieces and veils were artfully displayed inside two ornate white cabinets.

Taylor hovered at his side. "We try to cater for all types of occasions and give brides an idea of what's available. It helps them choose."

"What about the grooms? Don't they get a look in?"

"Of course. It's their day too. But usually what we find is the bride, and often her family, gets things underway."

"And the groom comes screaming up the rear?" Cade couldn't help himself. "Sorry." He shrugged sheepishly. "Marriage isn't in my line of thinking. I've seen how it works."

"Yet you attended your friend's wedding—even as best man," she countered, buttoning up her jacket, a reaction that definitely said keep away.

"I don't criticize others for wanting to give it a go. What do they say? Love is blind?" But as far as he was concerned, love was too risky. "Why bother with all this stuff?" he said, pointing to the bridal accoutrements about the room. "The divorce rate is here to stay. Of the twenty thousand odd marriages a year, virtually half that number end in divorce."

Taylor's mouth pursed. "My, you're a fistful of facts and figures, aren't you? Got any more you can spout off?"

"Nope, just those," he said, giving her his best disarming smile.

"I see."

He watched a flurry of emotions skitter across her eyes. They'd darkened to a deep ocean blue. "And what precisely is it you see? You going to get all uppity on me?"

"No." But she didn't quite look him in the eye. "Your attitude and the fact you can reel off facts and figures makes sense, though."

Cade frowned. What did she know about him?

He didn't like the way this was heading, and certainly didn't want some woman trying to get the better of him. "Taylor," he said, planting his feet firm, towering over her. "Let's get this straight. Don't try to analyze me."

"As if I would." She looked at him from beneath those long, dark lashes of hers.

Blast it. It sent his pulse skyrocketing and his thoughts scattering. Hell, one look like that and she could analyze all she wanted. "You might do it all the time for your clients, but I'm not a client."

"For your new bar concept you are."

"Yes, but not a marriage client. So enough of the psychobabble. My psyche isn't up for discussion."

"Suit yourself."

"You bet I will. Come on, let's go." Cade turned to walk away.

"To your new premises?"

"Yep, unless you want to try to analyze why I've started that venture too. If so, then let me tell you, this little deal of yours is O-F-F. Got it?"

Taylor saluted and grinned at him. "Yes, sir." She gathered a folder and builder's tape.

Round one to…him?

No way. Cade might have managed to forestall Taylor's analytical bent, but it wasn't over. Not by a long shot. And that, he realized, with a gnawing in the pit of his belly, was decidedly disconcerting.

He watched her move around the office. So sure of herself, like a gazelle, all long limbs and fluid motion. With her hair swept up in a French roll exposing her slender neck, he had the urge to kiss it and let his tongue slide across her exquisite skin.

Earlobes were an aphrodisiac, an erogenous zone. He'd like to find out how Taylor would react.

He'd been so sure it would be different away from the bar, without the ribald input from his customers and snoopy Miss Sister. But nothing had changed. The moment he walked into Taylor's office, he could smell her enticing perfume.

It hit him like a thunderbolt and tested his reserve.

Finally, he escaped outside, but with Taylor beside him, escape really was futile.

He'd brought the pickup this time. The pearlescent blue paintwork sparkled in the autumn sunlight. Cade held the door open for her.

"Showing off, Cade?"

"Now why would you say that?"

"Different car every day. Makes a man look successful."

"You called it showing off."

"So I did," she said, smiling up at him.

Witch. She was a teasing witch, but didn't even know it. He wanted to kiss that smile. He gripped the door handle with white-knuckle intensity. Anything to stop his brain thinking those thoughts...thoughts of what he'd like to do with Taylor right here and now. He gritted his teeth. "I simply thought since you like classic cars, you'd like this one." This really wasn't going to be easy.

Seated beside Taylor, he fired the ignition and eased the vehicle into the traffic.

"You promised to take me up and see your...etchings."

Yes! "So I did. Plenty of time." Now why the heck did he go and say that?

"Really?"

"Yeah, like I said, take it slow and easy."

Mate, you've lost it. What's happened to the wham, bam, thank you ma'am guy?

"Think of today as verbal foreplay," he said and saw Taylor's wide-eyed shock. He chuckled to himself. He was sure he'd heard her gulp too.

That was better. He felt in control now.

Slow and easy.

Just the sound of Cade's voice, languid and heavy, sent Taylor's hormones into an uproar.

Grateful that Cade had switched the radio to a rock station so she didn't have to find her voice, she watched his fingers tapping against the steering wheel. She was hypnotized, unable to submerge the thrill of wondering what his fingers would feel like against her skin.

Like sin.

A soporific sigh slid from her lips.

He gave her a curious glance. "You say something?"

"No. Just a bit tired, I guess."

"Another sleepless night?"

She twisted round sharply, only to catch Cade's knowing grin.

"Me too."

So why don't you do something about it? she moaned silently. *Put me out of my agony.*

Chapter Six

Cade's new premises were situated in the central business district, a part of the city that had seen a resurrection over the last few years. The gas works were gone, and the docks had morphed into a myriad of apartments and upscale shops and businesses.

He parked the pickup outside an old brick building with boarded windows and peeling paintwork.

In an instant, Taylor's mind whirred with ideas. Old and new, side by side. History and modern day.

Already out of the truck, Cade opened her door.

A perfect gentleman.

Captured by her surroundings, Taylor absently took Cade's hand as he helped her from the pickup. She didn't think—until that same tingling shot from her fingers up her arm, then her gaze snapped down to her hand, still in his, and she swallowed hard and shook her head.

Stumbling away, she pulled her hand from his.

Concentrate, Sullivan.

Refusing to look at Cade, she walked up to the building and cast her creative eye over the scuffed brickwork, the wrought iron handrails on either side of the well-worn steps. A knowing excitement bubbled up.

"I'm not sure I like the look on your face, Taylor. Give it to me. You think the place is a dump and won't work."

She turned to him and smiled. "No, it's wonderful. It's so evocative of Auckland's history."

"A pile of dilapidated bricks, you mean."

"Of course not. It's…"

"A dump," He finished for her.

"Definitely not."

A wary uncertainty crossed Cade's eyes. His countenance spoke silent volumes. This business venue meant more than dollars to him.

Pride?

She wouldn't damage that. Cade was going to give her something very important. She owed him her best efforts, refused to be put off by Cade's pessimism. "So there's quite a bit of work."

"Tell me about it. The builders are all ready to start."

"So I see." Scaffolding framed the façade, and workmen had already begun scraping back years of grime and neglect from the brickwork. Taylor trailed her fingers over the hand-hewn bricks, feeling their texture.

"You touch them as if they speak to you."

She smiled. Cade sounded worried. "They do in some ways," she confirmed. "It's sort of an intuition thing. They tell me what they want. A bit like a character in a book."

"Characters don't speak."

"They do to the writer, or at least that's what I've heard."

Obviously impatient, Cade jangled a clutch of keys from one hand. "Sounds nutty."

"Sounds exciting," she corrected.

"So, you approve of my purchase?"

Taylor grabbed his forearm and spun him round to face the front of the building. "Feel this, the age of it," she instructed. She lifted his hand, holding it in hers, and ran his fingers along the mottled bricks. "This building has seen so much and so many pass it. It has a sense of history, of pride of place in this city of ours. See the door? Okay, so graffiti has marred its elegance, but a bit of cleaning and it will be back to its stately proportions."

"You feel all this from touch?"

Taylor's head tilted to one side, and she searched his face. "Don't you?"

"Uh...I suppose."

"It's not simply touch, but all the senses. Sight, sound, smell, touch and, yes, probably even taste. We're close to where the fishing boats used to moor and deposit their catch, so the smell of salt and fish is integral to the building and its history. It's all there. We just have to pull it from the building's past."

But Cade obviously thought her nuts, and Taylor slammed her lips firmly closed. She shrugged, giving him an impish sort of grin.

"You trying to get me in touch with my softer side, Taylor? It's bricks and mortar. Dollars and cents. Nothing else. At least so my bank manager keeps reminding me."

Taylor wagged her finger at him. "Where's your romance?"

"Don't have any. Told you that."

"Yes, you do."

The air between them hung heavy with innuendo. Cade tightened his grip on her fingers. Her breathing stopped, and hot became scorching as he brought her fingertips to his parted lips, just touching. The warm wash of his breath fluttered against their tips, and Taylor's expectation surged.

Then he kissed them.

One fingertip at a time.

Slowly.

And Cade looked right into her soul.

"Never confuse business with pleasure, Ms. Sullivan."

With that, he dropped her hand and stuck the key in the antiquated lock, turning it under protest. Shoulder to the door, he pushed it open and strode into the abyss, leaving a shocked Taylor to follow.

Cade circled the vast space and walked to the nearest wall. Reaching out, he ripped a piece of tattered wallpaper off in one long, single tear and held it up to her. "Welcome to my empire. What do you want to know?"

Taylor's insides were pitted against each other in a conflict for control, when what she wanted to do was to reach out to him. Touch him.

She hid her hands behind her back, locking her fingers to prevent their shaking. Eying the room, she slowly counted to ten, knowing she needed to remain calm.

"What game are you playing, Cade? One minute you're all hot..."

"Hot, as in sexy?"

"Don't put me off. You know exactly what I mean. You're playing sex games."

"And you have a problem with this?"

Yeah, but she wouldn't admit to him she was scared witless.

"The next, you're as cold as ice—in the emotional sense. I don't know if I'm up to this anymore. Let's forget the deal."

"No!" Cade's shout echoed through the derelict building. "You can't. We can't."

"Of course we can," Taylor reasoned. "It's not a legal deal, nothing formal."

Cade reached out and caught her elbow, turning her to him and pulling her close—so close she could hear his breathing, see the flash of gold in his darkened gaze. "How can you disappoint your clients?" he challenged.

"Low blow." And damn it, she felt cornered. One part of her wanted to run for the hills, while the other part of her wanted to jump his bones, right there, right then. Her thoughts returned to the repeated phone calls, the desperate pleas of her brides.

Her knees wobbled, and she sank onto an upended crate, dust and cobwebs tangling with her bare legs. She looked up at Cade, and her heart skipped several beats.

You can do this.

Keep things business-like, she reminded herself.

"What have you got in mind?"

"That would be telling, but from the look of you," he said and gave her a direct stare, "I think business before pleasure."

Taylor's jaw dropped. "Can you read minds?"

"Depends on what you're thinking. If it's as wicked as what I'm thinking, we could be in for lots of fun," he said, winking. "Come on." He grabbed her hand, lacing his fingers through hers, and tugged slightly when she resisted.

But only a fraction. She could never resist him too long. And that scared her more than she cared to admit.

"The building," Cade informed her as he offered a guided tour, "consists of about a half dozen rooms. The main one will be used for the cocktail bar, while several of the smaller ones will be for private parties and corporate events."

"Do you have a theme?"

Cade frowned, then his expression turned to horrified, and Taylor choked back a fit of laughter.

"You mean like those weddings you plan?"

"Don't panic. I won't cover the place in miles of pink tulle or too much frou-frou."

"Who said I was panicking?"

"Your face says it all."

"You mean you can read me like a book?"

She wished.

"If that's the case, I better watch out. A man's gotta have some mystery."

The playful banter was fun—as if she'd known him for years, not a couple of days.

"Come on, there's more." Cade directed her toward a staircase to the right of the main door. As they drew alongside it, he ran a hand over the carved mahogany banister. "This is beautiful. True craftsmanship," he said, brushing the dust aside to reveal the still-smooth ambience of the dark wood.

"See," Taylor joked, "there is an itty bit of romance in that heart of yours, after all."

He shrugged and gave her one of those smiles again; the ones that set her heart thumping and her body wanting. "Could be."

An hour later, Taylor closed her folder on the screeds of notes she'd made.

"You got enough information?"

"I hope so. I can always come back."

"Sure. Anytime."

Cade might have agreed, but Taylor wasn't so sure

"anytime" was a good idea. *Anytime* changed business to pleasure, somehow.

She peered through the dust-coated window at a day divested of sunshine. The streetlights had switched on, and the ever-present sound of city traffic had reduced considerably.

"You hungry?" Cade asked as they wound their way back toward the head of the stairs.

"An ox wouldn't go amiss," she said, realizing the gnawing in her stomach wasn't nerves, but hunger.

"Not sure I can rustle up an ox, but the take-out joint next door does the best fish and chips I've ever had."

"Better than Hammerheads?"

Cade pretended to think a bit on that. "Let's just say different, a casual ambiance." He pulled his mobile phone from his pocket, punched in a couple of numbers and began listing off an order.

"You ordering for a football team?"

"I'm a hungry boy. Need feeding if I'm going to perform."

Perform?

Taylor stared wide-eyed at Cade. His eyes twinkled and he looked so good, so relaxed and happy.

Just so darn sexy, don't you mean?

Her belly did another round of flip-flops. Oh, Lordy.

"Dinner is superb," Taylor said as she grabbed another piece of mouthwatering battered fish. She licked a drop of sauce off her fingers.

"Best linens and best dinnerware too." Using the edge of his key ring, Cade flicked the lids off a couple of bottles of ice-cold beers and passed one to her.

"Fish and chips in paper *is* the best," she agreed.

"Don't forget the ketchup and a beer." He saluted her with his beer.

"Cheers. To...us."

"Yeah, to us. To wedding planners."

"And bar owners too," Taylor added, laughing.

Cade lifted the bottle to his mouth and took a swig of beer. Taylor watched him swallow, the way his Adam's apple bulged, how he wiped the tip of his tongue over his lips.

As he lowered his drink, his gaze leveled with hers. "To good old sex," he said.

Heat charged through Taylor's veins. She never knew drinking beer and eating a takeaway could be so sexy. Taking several fries, she dipped them in the sauce sachet. "Childhood memories are made of this. And new memories," she said, munching on the fries. This was one of those moments, one of the unforgettable ones that would stay with her—all night long.

"You reckon?"

"Uh-huh. Well not the 'good old sex' part," she said, blushing, "but you know, memorable meals and all that." She forced herself to continue, knowing Cade's gaze rested on her. "I remember when we were kids, my siblings and I would have fish and chips on a Friday night. Mum said it was her night off."

"She cooked every night?"

"Of course."

"Lucky you."

Taylor caught the change in Cade's tone, giving her reason to wonder about his childhood and family.

For a few minutes they ate in silence. They had set themselves a picnic spot against one wall. Cade leant back, long, jean clad legs stretched out. His T-shirt with the Ford logo and a revved up hotrod emblazoned across his chest delineated his muscled body beneath.

"Real boy's toy stuff," Taylor said, pointing to his chest.

"Yeah. Man's gotta have his passions."

"Um...I suppose so."

"What about yours?"

"Mine?" Taylor stared at the beer in her hands and twirled the bottle.

"You trying to play spin the bottle? There's just the two of us, so it could be interesting."

Her breathing slowed, and her lips parted. They were suddenly very dry.

Let's play?

Expectation fired in every part of her. She'd played that teen game before—with disastrous consequences.

"Once was enough, thank you very much," she forced out.

"Was it? This is getting interesting. When did you play spin the bottle?"

Taylor wiped the tip of her tongue over her parched lips, wishing the memories that ripped through her brain would just go away and leave her alone. Her heart palpitated and sweat slid between her shoulder blades. She blinked—once, twice, and then squeezed her eyes closed for a second. Finally, she spoke. "I was fifteen."

"First party?"

His intuition caught Taylor unawares. "You guessed right."

"Just lucky." He shrugged. "Or, more to the point, remembering back to my own first time. I guess it wasn't a fun night."

Taylor grimaced. "That's about it. It was the first time I'd been invited to a party. With my brain box family, I wasn't the most popular kid in school." Taylor trailed a nail along an imaginary pattern in her dress—remembering it all over again. "Those days seem so far away, yet like yesterday," she said sadly. "Bobby Harcourt asked me."

"The coolest boy in school?"

Her finger halted its course. "Most of the girls thought so."

"And you?"

"I felt...lucky, privileged that he'd ask out the school nerd."

"And?"

"It was a disaster from the minute I walked in. The music was so loud I couldn't hear a word, or think."

He chuckled. "Careful, you're showing your age."

Taylor offered him a tentative smile. "Probably, but back then I felt so out of my depth." Exactly like now, she reasoned. "It seemed as if the whole school arrived. The so-called adult supervision my father had remonstrated about turned out to be an older sister—older by about two years. She just wanted to have fun."

"What happened?"

"Drugs and booze, sex in the bathroom. You name it. It happened. Everywhere I looked, something was going on," she whispered. "So I left. Fast. The next morning when my parents found out about the party, I was grounded for a month."

"But you didn't do anything."

"No. I was the proverbial good girl, just like you said." She lifted her chin and stared at him. "Ms. Prim, I think you called me."

He gave her a sheepish grin. "Oops."

"No, you're right. I was then, and...well, I suppose I am now too." But what she hadn't told Cade was that she'd run scared—emotionally and for some psycho reason, she'd taken sanctuary in the security of what she knew. Who she knew. In Rob.

Outside, the blast of a car horn pierced the silent streets and brought reality back with a thud.

All those years ago. Not so different now.

Yes, it is.

It was. Really. Now she was smack bang in the middle of cutting the apron strings to that sanctuary, and it scared the heck out of her. For some reason she had held on to the notion that she needed her family's approval.

Not now. Now she wanted that freedom. And she would grab it.

Taylor finished her beer and put down the bottle. "My turn now."

His eyes narrowed on her. "Didn't know this was a turnabout."

"Humor me," she said. Though what she really wanted wasn't chitchat but *action*. Sitting with Cade, talking about emotions and passions wrapped Taylor in an intimacy so real her body hummed with an aching need. A need that required massaging. If she dared.

"You want to know the man before you have sex with him?"

"Better late than never," she said, trying for humor. "Or are you aiming to get out of talking? How like a man."

"And you're an expert?"

"Scared?" she shot back.

One dark brow arched. "Of what?"

What was she thinking? Cade Harper, scared? Never in a million years. The man oozed confidence. "Try communicating," she offered, saying the first thing she could think of. It hit the mark.

For a moment, his gaze shifted away and time stood still, the silence deafening. Shifting uncomfortably on her dusty, upturned box, Taylor bent and retrieved her bottle from the scuffed floor. She took a sip, enjoying the tangy froth as it slid down her throat, succoring her dry lips, then replaced the bottle. She rested her hands on her hips. "Waiting," she prompted him.

"You're very determined, aren't you?"

"When it's something I want." But the moment those words passed Taylor's lips, she witnessed his reaction and cringed.

And you want me, he said.

Taylor snatched up her beer and drank thirstily, draining its contents.

An icy droplet trickled down her chin. She went to brush it off, but Cade reached out to her.

"Let me." His voice was warm, and his darkened gaze burned into her as he brushed away the drop.

Time seemed to stand still.

Then he did something that sent her over the edge. He licked the tiny drop from his fingers. Slowly. An act so intimate and blatant it left her in no doubt as to what Cade wanted. Hypnotized, she watched the tip of his tongue slide over each of his fingers, sucking, tasting.

Oh, dear heaven. Taylor squeezed her knees together as slick moistness pooled between her thighs and shivery tingles chased each other up and down her spine.

Talk.

Talk for goodness sake.

Think of something, anything.

Taylor swallowed hard. "How did you end up owning the bar?" she asked, the words coming out in a breathless rush.

"That's bars, plural," Cade admitted easily.

"Really? Very impressive."

"Glad you think so."

"You're very sure of yourself, aren't you?"

"Why not? If I don't blow my own trumpet, no one will do it for me. You're in business. You should know that."

"Do you need to blow it?"

"It helps." He shrugged and downed the last of his beer.

Taylor watched as he swallowed, his full lips pursed around the bottle opening, the way he wiped a droplet of beer from his mouth with the back of his hand. A simple act, yet one she found erotic in the extreme.

She wanted to reach out and stop him.

She wanted to taste it. Taste him.

Finally, she found her tongue. "How does it help?"

"What is this—twenty questions?"

"No. Just trying to get to know you, return the interrogation favor."

You're trying to prolong the inevitable. Scaredy cat.

Cade's dark eyes rolled toward the heavens. "Am I so interesting?"

"Don't get a swollen head." She laughed. "It's simple interest, that's all."

"Why is it women want to get all chatty?"

"You mean instead of getting down and dirty."

"Yeah, well, that's a different angle," he agreed, grinning.

"Talk about a wolf in sheep's clothing. Wasn't it you who said we should take it easy?"

Cade's eyes rolled again. "Is this that Venus and Mars stuff? You know, the men versus women speak? Just so you understand, I don't talk about myself."

"Why not?"

He let out a long, slow whistle. "You don't give up, do you?"

She shrugged. The air hung thick between them, and once again she chastised herself. Everyone told her to get a life. To live. But...she couldn't. Not properly.

Everyone expected things of her. Her family. Even, somehow—a dead fiancé.

"I left school at sixteen," Cade said, his voice ringing out in the silence.

She reached over and touched a hand to his forearm. "You don't have to."

He wrapped his fingers over hers. "I know I don't. But somehow, with you, it's easier."

"I'm glad." And she was. Perhaps if Cade could open up a little, she might be able to subdue her doubts. She'd asked him a big favor. It was the delivery, however, that was setting her on edge.

He still held her hand in his, thumb caressing the back of her hand. She didn't pull it away. It felt right. Actually, it felt more than that. It felt *good*.

He continued. "Mostly I took on odd jobs, building and laboring. I had a head for figures, loved maths at school."

Taylor screwed her nose up at that. "Lucky you. Maths was my worst subject, and try telling that to parents who were mathematicians."

"Really?"

"Didn't go down very well, that's for sure."

"That I can believe."

"Go on. What next?"

"I did some work for a developer, had a few dollars put aside and found the property in Devonport."

"So that's your flagship bar, so to speak?"

"Yeah. Then there are a couple here in the city, one in the CBD and the other along the waterfront where they have the Sunday markets."

"Good locations."

"Location is everything."

"So they say," she agreed. "What about your family?"

But the mention of his family changed Cade. It was as if a shield came down and he'd donned a coat of armor. The bright fire burning in his eyes evaporated, replaced by a gloomy sadness. His fingers stilled their teasing stroke.

"You've met Katie. Then there's Zane. He's two years younger than me."

"And your parents?"

"Dad's somewhere down south."

"And your mother?" she coaxed.

Cade shrugged, seemingly nonchalant, but a flush stained his cheeks and the sadness in his eyes darkened.

"That's it. That's enough." He hauled himself to his feet and kicked at a derelict piece of wood. The wood clattered across the concrete floor, spinning out of control.

He walked away, his back hunched, hands deep in his pockets.

Unsure what to do, she scooped up the remains of their meal and looked around for a rubbish bin. There was nothing in sight, so she headed for the door, about to exit the building when Cade called her name.

"Taylor, don't go. I'm…sorry."

Her hand dropped from the door, and she turned to face him, surprised he stood so close.

Too close.

So close, she could reach out and touch him. She wanted to. Wanted to ease the pain she saw etched in his darkened eyes and brush away the furrows in his brow.

Cade took their leftovers from her and tossed them into an empty metal drum to his right. "I'm sorry," he repeated. "It's all this questioning. I'm not used to it."

"You said let's go slow. I was doing that,"

"I know. It's not you. It's me. It…oh, hell, Taylor, it is you."

Taylor's heart thudded to a halt.

"You walked into my bar and everything went up in smoke. I want you, more than I care to admit."

"And that's a bad thing?"

"Yeah. Sad but true. Okay, I admit it, I'm screwed up, but I don't want commitment."

"We've gone through this. Neither do I."

He reached for her hands, fingers looped around her wrists. The room seemed to have shrunk. It was just her and Cade. One on one.

He looked at her mouth. "I know."

Kiss me. Go on. Do it! Please.

Taylor fought for sanity. "It's only once. A one-nighter."

"Teacher and student," he replied with a hint of humor returning.

A shuddering breath rippled from Taylor's lips, and she arched toward him.

"You are very beautiful."

She tried to breathe. Nope. Not a hope in Hades. "Every woman loves to hear those words."

"You wanted fire, sweetheart. You've got it."

Cade's mouth claimed hers. Hot. Demanding. And very delicious.

Oh, Lordy, he was kissing her. At last.

He pressed his body hard up against her, and the door claimed her back.

So beautiful," he murmured as his tongue danced a sensual tango with hers.

She could feel him. All of him. His broad chest brushed against her breasts, enticing her nipples into rock hard nubs, and when his hips pressed against hers, his arousal rubbed against her belly.

Oh, God, she wanted him.

A sound rippled through the air—a sultry cry of need. Taylor realized it was her own voice. She fixed Cade with a direct gaze. "Is this that mood you talked about?"

"Sweetheart, do you doubt it?"

Heat rolled through Taylor at breakneck speed.

Doubt? She had none.

Cade's lips sealed over hers once more, his skilful hands spanning her waist, sliding upward in a teasing path. He reached her breasts, and his thumbs circled her nipples, tempting her beyond endurance.

Her head rolled back and exposed her neck, eliciting a groan of pleasure from Cade. "I've waited for this. Now I know."

"Know what?"

"What you taste like," he murmured as his lips sought solace along her neck. "It's true. Necks are oh-so-very erogenous."

With his dark eyes shrouded by long, inky lashes, he looked dangerous and very sexy. Just looking at him fired Taylor's emotions, emotions she wasn't sure she understood.

She brushed them aside. She didn't want to think. Simply to feel. Feel Cade's touch. And she wasn't disappointed.

He found the zip of her dress and effortlessly slid it down.

"You've had practice."

"Makes perfect. And you, sweetheart, are perfect."

As he eased the straps of her dress down her shoulders, anticipation fueled her senses, and her mouth went dry. Her eyes widened as she watched Cade's burning expression focus on her.

"Well, well." He grinned. "Miss Prim is a real surprise," he said as one hand traced the lacy outline of her bra.

Lace and silk. Sexy and sinful. Her secret.

"Who would have known that you wore such tempting concoctions beneath your prim little clothes?"

Cade stepped back and let out a long wolf-whistle as his gaze slid down her length. Slowly. Hungrily. It was as if he ate her up—whole. "Baby. That sure is something." His gaze slid lower—to her thong—and Taylor's body zinged alive. Hotter than hot.

She should have been embarrassed. No man had seen her this undressed before, and swimwear didn't count.

Cade liked what he saw. Obviously. His arousal pressed hard against his jeans, and his heavy hooded gaze burned with desire. Just the thought of it made Taylor feel—powerful. She'd never felt that before.

"If you keep looking at me like that, I won't be able to stay in control."

"Who said I wanted control?" she countered.

A flicker of surprise passed across Cade's eyes seconds before he pulled her to him. She came up hard, air stalling in her lungs.

He kissed her. Again.

And again and again.

On her lips, her eyelids, her cheeks. Everywhere.

And Taylor kissed him right back. She wanted his kisses. Lots of them. Every single one. And more.

She wasn't sure she could breathe. But the moment Cade's warm fingers unclipped her bra and the scrap of garment fell away, she knew breathing wasn't important.

He cupped a breast in each hand, lowered his mouth and sucked one then the other. Back and forth, over and deliciously over, while Taylor floated in a glorious heaven and swallowed a throaty cry of sinful pleasure.

Her fumbling fingers found the hem of Cade's T-shirt and burrowed beneath. She rejoiced as she trailed them over his skin. Ridges, angles and his wiry hair slid beneath her fingertips. Everything was new, a sensory exploration that delighted her. She wanted more. She wanted to see Cade, just as he saw her. "Take your T-shirt off."

A broad grin lit his face. "Anything you command."

Taylor held her breath as he dragged the T-shirt over his head.

Tanned skin and hard muscles didn't disappoint.

"If you keep looking at me like that, I'll think you want something."

"I do. I want to touch too."

"Go right ahead."

Again her voice sounded sultry. Sexy, even. Taylor wondered where it had come from. Had she been this woman all along, simply suppressed? Or was it Cade's doing?

She splayed her hands across his torso, feeling the rise and fall of his ribs and the thud of his heartbeat pounding beneath her fingertips. That simple action elicited a smile from her. That his heartbeat raced like her own delighted her.

Empowered, Taylor tugged gently at his curling hair, ran her fingers across his nipples, wondering at their darkened texture and color. She stole a tentative glance at Cade. Suddenly, she wasn't so sure. "Am I doing this wrong? I've..."

"Sweetheart, nothing you do could be wrong," he answered in a voice laced with desire. "Don't stop. You have my permission to take as long as you like, and then some."

Temptation proved too strong, and her fingers began a dance across his skin. Everything was about the senses. The touch of his skin against hers, feeling the rise and fall of his chest, his breath warm and teasing and the tiny groans she elicited from him as she found each pleasure spot.

She smiled, filled with joy that she could cause such rapture.

Then there was taste. Taylor wiped the tip of her tongue across her bottom lip, saw his gaze follow her every movement. Her vision blurred momentarily as she focused on the thrust of his arousal.

A single drop of perspiration curled its way down Cade's chest. Taylor leant forward.

She inhaled. He smelt so good.

Hot. All male. Hers.

The droplet inched its way down his abdomen—lower—until it circled the dip of his belly button.

It was hers. With the tip of her tongue, Taylor licked the droplet, tasting it, relishing it.

"Delicious."

A thick throaty moan of rapture ripped from Cade's throat. "Ain't that the truth."

Taylor smiled. Cade was definitely struggling for control. "This is better than chocolate," she laughed, licking his skin. "It tastes salty, hot and..." She purred and looked at him through the veil of her hair. "Very sexy."

"Enough. My turn." Cade gripped her wrists and pulled her against him, hooking one of her legs over his hip so she was spread wide. With one hand cupping her bottom, his fingers kneaded her flesh. They were warm and teasing, inciting a need in Taylor so strong she thought she would burst.

The moment his fingers grazed across her thong, feeling her wetness, her excitement spiraled and her eyelids fluttered closed. Cade's tantalizing touch was sending her to another world.

"Good?"

She nodded. She couldn't speak. But, oh, boy, she could feel. Cade's fingers brushed her secret place, a place no other had ever touched. It felt so right, and that it was Cade somehow made it perfect. She lost all sense of time, every part of her centered on one spot.

"I didn't know..." She moaned as the pleasure intensified.

"Know what, sweetheart?"

"That it could be so..." Her mind in a hypnotic haze of lust and need, Taylor struggled to find the right word. Any word. Then she knew exactly what it was. How it was. "Exquisite."

"It only gets better."

And it did. His lips trailed down her neck, dotting butterfly kisses that were so gentle, yet sexier and more teasing than anything she'd ever experienced.

He slipped a finger beneath the thin sheath and glided it across her moist core.

Taylor's breath stalled, and her eyes flashed open, speared by Cade's dark, heat-fuelled stare. Her stomach clenched, and a strangled gasp rent the air.

Her gasp.

He instantly stilled and retreated.

Don't stop.

But it was already too late. He stepped back and the moment, the beautiful, delicious moment when her body hummed with need for him, his touch, his kisses, the way he played her, bringing her alive, disintegrated. Taylor had never felt such a sense of abandonment.

Face flushed and eyes hooded, Cade dragged a hand through his hair. But he couldn't dilute the desire she saw still mirrored in his narrowed gaze.

"Cover up, Taylor," he bit out.

"But..."

"Please." He turned from her and stalked to the other side of the room.

Vulnerable in her half-dressed state, Taylor shivered as an icy sadness slid down her spine. Quickly, she hooked her bra and dragged her dress back up, but as she went to pull the zip, it snagged.

She yanked at it. And again. It wouldn't budge.

Cade stood a few feet away, but the distance could have been miles, his expression making it clear he was lost in his own world of recriminations. He didn't look at her.

"Cade?"

"Yes." He sounded so weary as he turned to her, his expression guarded. He kept his gaze focused no lower than her face.

"I have a problem. My zip is stuck."

For a moment, he looked at her as if he didn't understand, then realization colored his eyes to the darkest of chocolate. "Turn around," he instructed sharply.

Hugging her hands across her chest, Taylor did as she was told. And waited. For several long, drawn out moments, he didn't move, remaining silent.

Goose bumps skittered across her bare skin, and she shivered. "Cade?"

"I can't."

Taylor frowned. "Is it broken?" she asked. "Blast, the dress is fairly new."

With a gentle tug, the zip slid up effortlessly, and Taylor turned to face him. She stood so close his body heat wrapped around her. She hugged her arms across her middle.

"Can't what? You've fixed the zip. Thank you."

A hint of a smile teased his hard face, then disappeared a second later. "We can't."

An arctic chill iced her veins, her understanding instant. She stiffened and pulled away. "I think you've said enough."

She hurt. Damn it. Deep down inside. A place where no one could see except her. Mortified at her stupidity for letting go, for being such an easy target, Taylor gathered up her bag and folder of notes and walked to the door.

"I'm doing this all wrong."

She spun round on her heels, fury firing every part of her. "What's wrong, Cade, is that *you* are a tease. You stop and start at will."

"I just said not here, that's all."

"That's all? That wasn't exactly what you said. What you

said was—you can't," she parroted with sarcasm. "Once again you've started something you didn't finish."

Several, loud harsh seconds ticked by, and with each one, Taylor fought to harden her heart.

"You think I don't intend to finish what we started?"

"You have a habit of that where I'm concerned it seems. But it's okay. I'm letting you off the hook." Taylor yanked open the door. She had to get out of there.

Damn, damn, damn. She'd been stupid and let her emotions get the better of her, trusted herself. How dumb was that? She'd trusted her emotions once before, only to realize she'd been making a huge mistake.

"I'm not putting myself through this again. I can't. Too bad if my clients want to know about orgasms and sexual positions. I'll refer them to the library."

"Taylor?"

She held up a hand to stall him. "I don't deserve this."

"No, you don't."

She squeezed her eyes closed and battled to hold back the tears but failed. One after another they cascaded down her cheeks, an unstoppable flow, which only intensified her anger—at herself.

"You deserve better, Taylor. You don't deserve some derelict building and a stack of dusty cushions on a rubbish-strewn floor."

She opened her eyes and roughly brushed at her dampened cheeks. Cade stood in front of her. She could lean forward and kiss him. She wanted to. Very much.

No, you don't.

Oh, yes, she did.

Her jaw stiffened as she held firm, confused by the

intensity of her feelings for this man, a virtual stranger. Nothing could douse the heat and lust and...yearning she felt for him. She still wanted him. Yet her brain warned her to tread carefully. Not to get hurt.

Too late.

Cade finally spoke, ending the silence. "You asked something very special of me the other night. A privilege most men never get asked. I don't want you to remember your first time surrounded by dirt and debris. I want you. Hell, you've got me hot, sweetheart. Don't think this business is finished."

"It isn't?"

His fingers cupped her chin, tilting it upward, and he speared her with a blistering gaze. "Far from it, sweetheart." He slid a hand over hers, linking their fingers. "Come on. Let's go."

Taylor stalled. "Where to?"

"To unfinished business."

Chapter Seven

"What is it they say about best laid plans?" Taylor chuckled as they exited the building and witnessed Cade's excitement...not just for her, but for the row upon row of vintage and classic cars that lined the street.

Cade slapped a hand to his forehead. "Damn it. I forgot."

"What?"

He waved toward the cars lined along the kerb. "It's All American Night. Every month, owners of American hot rods and classic cars meet up here, then drive through the city along the waterfront. But mostly it's a chance for owners to browse around."

"And drool," Taylor said, laughing.

Cade's mouth quirked into an impish grin, gaze feasting on chrome and spectacular paint jobs. "I guess."

"So let's go drool," she urged.

"But we're meant to be doing...stuff?"

"It can wait, Cade. The cars are beautiful."

Cade gave her a quick smile. He drew her toward him. "Have I told you you're beautiful too?"

"A few minutes ago," she said and gloried in the desire she saw mirrored in Cade's dark gaze. "But I don't mind if you say it again," she answered truthfully, and laughed aloud, surprised and delighted to hear her own laughter. She couldn't remember the last time she'd felt so relaxed, so joyful. Cade's mouth found hers, and she leaned against him, amazed at how a mouth could feel so delicious and give so much joy as Cade's did to her.

"The cars," she reminded him.

"Hmm, but this is yummy."

"You make me sound like chocolate."

"Yeah. Rich caramel chocolate, the Swiss kind, the stuff that melts in your mouth. Far too good to miss."

"You won't miss it," she said, pulling back. "It's just on delayed time, that's all."

"Promise?"

"Absolutely."

"I'll hold you to that."

"I'll make sure you do," she countered. Yep. She sure would.

Hand in hand, they strolled along the sidewalk, Taylor leaning into Cade's embrace as they viewed the long line of cars. It felt so good to be with him. Normal, in fact. All around them, people talked, admired the cars, the atmosphere almost carnival-like.

"Oh, look. Cotton candy." Taylor's mouth watered as she pointed toward a group of stallholders selling the bright pink confectionery along with toffee apples and hot fries. "We could call it dessert."

"And here I was thinking *you* were dessert," Cade said, kissing her again.

"Do you want whipped cream with that?"

Cade let out a low belly rumble. "Don't tempt me." He

bowed regally, humor dancing across his expressive face. "Madam, dessert awaits." He directed her toward the closest stall. "Two, please."

The vendor passed over the cotton candy, and Cade paid. He held them out. "You've a choice. Pink or pink."

"Oh, pink, I think."

As they carried on through the crowd, Cade delighted in informing her about each vehicle, its make and year.

"You're a mine of information, aren't you?" she said, truly impressed.

"I try."

"You're succeeding."

They came upon a group huddled around two cars. Taylor couldn't hold back her sudden excitement. "I know these ones. That's a '55 Chevy." She pointed toward the car. "And that bike is a Triumph Bonneville, the Jaguar of bikes. I thought you said this was for American cars."

"It is, but really it's just for out and out petrol heads." Cade's brows rose. "So how do you know all this stuff?"

"I told you, I'm a petrol head in disguise."

"It's more than that. That year car and the bike are quite rare. What aren't you telling me, Taylor?"

A frisson of panic skittered up and down Taylor's spine. "Nothing," she denied instantly. She pulled her arm from his and put some space between them. "You're making something out of nothing."

"No, I'm not. I bet most of the people here wouldn't know that bike or the Chevy."

"So I read car magazines in my spare time." Taylor wished with all her heart Cade would drop the subject. She didn't want to dredge up memories. Rob had been too sick to tinker on his

'48 Ford, so instead she'd sat with him for hours, reading his car magazines to him—until death caught up.

Sudden, unbidden tears pricked at Taylor's eyes.

Damn. She didn't want to cry. Not now, and certainly not in front of Cade. She brushed them away. Rob was gone, and her feelings for him were confused, a mixture of guilt and a sadness that she'd made such a senseless and stupid error. Something that, even four years on, tested her judgment where men were concerned.

Standing with her back to the Chevy, Taylor watched Cade as he talked to a couple of other enthusiasts, the play of his strong face, the light that shone from his eyes when he was relaxed.

He was a good man. Thoughtful. Considerate. He'd been thinking of her when he'd stalled their lovemaking, not wanting her to experience sex in a derelict building.

That was kind. That was...well, it was simply Cade Harper.

A warmth pervaded Taylor's bones, sneaking up on her, cosseting and comforting. There was absolutely nothing simple about Cade.

She owed him an explanation, but there was no way she could actually put that explanation into words. How did she tell him she'd wanted to dump a dying fiancé?

It didn't sound good in any language.

"Taylor?"

Her head shot up as his voice snatched her back from the past. Cade stood so close, a little boy lost look on his face, all serious and sad.

A tentative smile curved her mouth. She wanted to reach out and touch him, brush away that sadness. "Do you always sneak up on a gal?"

"Only when it's you. I wanted to apologize," he said. His hands rested on her shoulders, and he pulled her to him. Taylor had to arch her neck back to look into his face, and when she did, she realized she was lost.

"What for?" she asked.

"The interrogation. It's not my business if you like cars. Though I must admit it's kinda sexy. Gives a guy fantasies."

Taylor's breath stalled, excitement coiling low down in her belly. "Fantasies. Hmm. Such as?"

"Do you really want to know?" One of Cade's hands trailed down her back, cupping her bottom. He steered her backwards, leaning her against the side of a nearby car. Taylor felt the car's hard metallic curves at the back of her legs. They parted, and Cade slid between them. She felt his arousal straining against his jeans pushing against her sex.

Here?

Blatant and very public.

Taylor didn't care. She wanted to feel all of him.

Cade slipped a hand between them and tugged at her nipple. It hardened beneath his touch.

"How about hot, fast sex? Here in the back of the car."

Taylor's eyes widened, heat flooding her cheeks, burning even her scalp.

Fantasies!

Her muscles tensed, relaxed, then tensed again with wanting him.

How did she know how it would feel? She had no experience. Yet she knew, absolutely, what Cade would feel like inside her—and she wanted it. Wanting it was killing her.

As Cade blew little kisses down the side of her neck, nuzzling her earlobe, her hands threaded through his hair. The texture of it spiked her senses, and a trembling sigh escaped her lips.

"Yes," she whispered against his ear.

Cade's hot sigh fanned her skin. "Then, I'd go slow. Tasting you, feeling you come around me, squeezing me. Hear those soft, mewing moans of pleasure you make."

Oh, boy.

Taylor leant against the car, felt the hard metal press into her back. She lifted one leg and hooked it around Cade's. He lifted her slightly, pressing himself harder against her, and kissed her. Deeply, thoroughly. Transporting her to another world. Her sex rubbed against him, and a surge of urgent need shot through every part of her. She felt reckless. Carnal.

In the background, the sound of wolf whistles fought through the fog of desire wrapped around her. Cade must have heard them too, and pulled back a fraction. "We need to get out of here."

Taylor's eyes fluttered open. For a moment, she was confused about where she was, then reality struck. "My God, in public. We were..." Her breathing came in short pants, and she pushed Cade away slightly. "I can't believe it. We were on..."

"Fire," Cade offered. "Both of us, Taylor. It wasn't just me. We both wanted it. Here. Right now."

"Oh, God." Taylor eyed Cade. She saw the stain of that very heat he talked about beneath his skin. She squeezed her eyes shut, blinking out reality. She couldn't believe it. She'd jumped his bones—in public. She'd been quite prepared to make love with him right here, right now.

How could she have been so stupid, so blind? So...she'd actually forgotten where she was. Cade made her forget.

"Come on."

"Where?" Taylor felt numb, a deliciously hot and sexy kind of numbness.

"Home. We've got that unfinished business, remember?"

They hadn't gone more than a few steps when someone called out Cade's name. "Hey, brother, hold up."

Cade let out a groan and muttered beneath his breath. He pulled on Taylor's hand and quickened his pace.

"Wait up." Their pursuer obviously wasn't giving up, Taylor realized.

A hand slapped Cade on the back, and he halted, fury creasing his brow. He turned one-eighty to face their interloper.

"Not now, Zane."

"Hey, is that a way to treat family?"

Zane? Cade's brother. Taylor eyed him. He looked like Cade. Softer, not as tall, but he still had those devilishly good looking Harper cheekbones.

"Aren't you going to introduce us?" Zane asked, looking directly at her.

"Nope. Gotta go." Cade tried to turn, but it was obvious Zane wasn't having any of that.

"I'm Zane, his younger brother," he said, holding out his hand.

Taylor took it, surprised when the younger Harper took her hand to his lips and kissed it.

"Mitts off, brother," Cade almost growled, surprising her by his he-man tactics.

"What? Can't stand a little competition?"

"You'd lose." Cade stood rigid. The tiny pulse in his jaw she'd come to recognize when he battled for control flickered a relentless beat.

"Wanna bet?"

"No contest." Cade wrapped a proprietary arm around Taylor's shoulder.

"Enough." She eased her hand from Zane's and wagged a finger at both men. "What is this? Sibling rivalry?"

"Brotherly love," Zane informed her. "Just checking up on the old boy here. Don't wear him out, now." And with that, Zane gave them a jaunty wink and wave and sauntered toward a group of young women.

For a few seconds, Cade remained immobile, his narrowed gaze fixed on the retreating Zane. Then he turned to her, a wash of concern coloring his face.

"Sorry about my brother. You okay?" Taylor nodded, but when she shivered, Cade shrugged off his leather jacket and draped it around her shoulders.

As surreptitiously as she could, she dipped her head, inhaling deeply the fragrance imbued into the leather. It smelled of Cade. All warm and masculine. Pulling the edges around her, she hugged it closer. Once again, it was just the two of them, the crowd fading into nothingness.

"We've a date, I believe."

Taylor's toes curled. "How could I forget?"

"I'd hoped you hadn't."

"That would be impossible where you're concerned, Mr. Harper."

"Good. Let's go." Linking his hand in hers, they almost ran back to where he'd parked the pickup. Cade gunned the engine as it roared to life. He gave her a quick glance. "You okay?"

Oh, yes. She was more than okay. She was definitely *ready*.

The moment Taylor stepped up behind Cade outside the bar's back entrance, any doubts she'd been harboring flew out the proverbial window.

He turned to her, a finger over his smiling lips. "We need to be quiet unless you want my nosey parker sister springing us." Draping his arms over her shoulders, Cade pulled her to him. She came up against his hard body. His very sexy body.

It felt good—again.

Excitement bubbled inside Taylor, and she reached up and kissed him softly on the lips.

"Do that again and I won't be able to control my actions," he murmured against her mouth.

"Is that a promise?" She kissed him again. There was nothing gentle or tentative about this kiss. She kissed him hard, stroking the side of his face, tasting him. Her hands slid beneath his T-shirt, his shudder as her fingertips splayed across his heated skin delighting her.

Breathless, she pulled back, witnessing Cade's reaction. And when he chuckled, the velvety, husky tone of his laughter sent shivers of need through her veins. "Come on, we need some privacy."

With as much stealth as any spy, Taylor followed him up the back stairs of the bar to his apartment.

Cade switched on a table lamp and a soft glow spread around the room.

It was a very manly sort of place. Leather couches and dark wood floors, a cream Flokati rug in front of an unlit fireplace. Topnotch sound systems and a large wall-mounted flat screen television identified the apartment as home to someone who knew technology.

But it was the shining chrome hubcap, with its bold V8 insignia hanging in pride of place above the fireplace that brought an instant smile to Taylor's lips.

Yes, this was Cade's home.

She was aware of Cade's scrutiny, though, and those dratted butterflies erupted again, dancing in her belly. But mostly she could still feel the moisture—down there—where Cade had teased her alive.

"Do you want a drink?"

She shook her head.

"Food?"

Heat flooded her cheeks, and she shook her head again. *Nope. Not that kind of food.*

She dropped her gaze.

"Taylor, what do you want?"

You. I want you, her brain shouted. Her body agreed wholeheartedly.

"Taylor? Speak to me. If you want to bow out and change your mind, I won't think badly of you."

"I don't. I haven't changed my mind."

She heard Cade's sigh of relief, and it boosted her flagging confidence.

Emboldened, she closed the gap between them and clasped Cade's hand in hers, lifting it to her lips. She took his middle finger and wiped it across her parted lips. Never once did her gaze leave his beautiful face.

Her tongue licked his fingertip. Once. Twice.

She sucked on it in such a primal way it could never leave Cade in doubt as to what she had in mind.

"You taste delicious," she whispered.

He tasted—of her. Oh, Lordy! A scalding heat burned right through her. She tasted herself.

Cade's cheeks dimpled and his smile broadened. The man had seen her shock. He knew *exactly* what she was thinking.

Cade knew he needed to slow down. He didn't want to scare Taylor, but heaven help him, she tempted him *so* badly.

Unspeaking, he reached up and brushed at a strand of her hair, winding it round his finger. The silken curl caressed his skin. His jaw tightened, and he swallowed back the urge to plunge into her moist depths, right there and then.

Take it easy, huh? Slow down. He felt as if a steamroller had ripped right over him. He didn't know what slow was anymore, whether he could even go slow, or wanted to.

With wide, innocent eyes, she looked up at him through unbelievably long lashes. Innocent?

What she did to him didn't even remotely feel innocent. It heated him to boiling point.

He felt a shiver ripple through her and smiled. "Do you know what you're doing to me?"

A tinkling sound of pure joy fell from her lips. "I think so."

His cheek caressed hers.

"What was that?"

"A butterfly kiss." He laughed.

"It tickled," she said of the tease of his lashes against her cheek.

Cade's laughter suddenly died. Kissing was serious business. "But this, this is a *real* kiss." And he swooped down on her mouth, savoring her taste, the feel of her mouth beneath his.

And it felt good.

Damned good.

He wanted more. He wanted to feel her tongue against him, just like when she sucked his fingers.

The tension in Cade spiraled as he teased her lips open and dipped into the sweet recess of her mouth.

"You wanted real," he murmured, not wanting to leave her mouth for one moment.

"And I got it." Her hands did seriously sexy things to his skin, rubbing across his nipples, tugging at them, and time lost importance. He dropped his hands to her waist. She was so small he could nearly span it. In one fluid movement, he unzipped her dress and went to pull down the straps.

"Wait." Her hand halted his movements. "Let me."

Cade didn't know how much more he could take.

She took a step back, reached up and clasped the straps of her dress in both hands, and, oh-so-very-slowly enough that Cade thought he'd died and gone to heaven, she began to strip.

She slid the straps down her arms first, lowering the dress, inch by glorious inch, keeping her gaze hooked on his, not wavering one iota.

His erection swelled, uncomfortable as it strained against his jeans. He needed release. He needed Taylor. Now.

He wanted to reach out and take her in his arms, finish the job, strip her bare, plunge into her delectable heat. But he didn't.

Damn it. Slow down.

He cursed his greedy need. He'd never felt like this about any woman, never needed to. He'd been the player, the one in control. But right now, Cade wasn't sure about anything.

"You want more?" she asked.

He found his tongue tied in knots, and he nodded like some pubescent schoolboy. Trouble was, he felt like one. Eager—and so very ready.

The dress descended, revealing first the firm swell of her breasts, just visible above that lacy concoction she called a bra. Then more.

He sucked in oxygen. Was he meant to breathe? Who cared? His gaze stuck fast to Taylor as the dress slid lower and lower, exposing her flat abdomen, the soft curve of her hips. She halted.

He wanted to call out, "No, don't stop. Keep going. I can't wait any longer."

She smiled at him. This woman had total control over him. She had from the moment she'd walked into the bar.

She hooked the straps of her sheath dress over her thumbs and still it slid lower. Cade's gaze went with the dress. His heart beat so frantically he was sure it would explode. Everything centered on Taylor.

The dress hit the floor, and she stepped out of it, kicking it aside with the tips of those sexy high heels of hers.

Beneath the soft lighting, she stood, dressed only in the underwear she'd surprised him with earlier—and heels. Heels that made her legs look as if they went on forever. Legs he imagined wrapped around him.

Cade sucked in his breath. "Beautiful."

And she was. A tumble of hair cascaded around her shoulders in a glorious cloud. There was a tempting peek of hardened nipples thrusting against her lacy bra. Taylor was an exquisite sight to behold.

His breath jammed in his lungs. He reached a hand out to her.

Would she come? Or would she back out? Taylor might have waited a long time for this moment, but Cade felt as if he'd waited a lifetime.

Chapter Eight

Taylor had made up her mind. There was no going back. She took Cade's hand and he led her toward the bedroom. He kicked the door open and went to switch on the light.

She stilled his hand. "No. Leave it off."

She saw his hesitation and could understand why. She'd just exhibited the most erotic striptease—and now she wanted the light off.

"Please." Her plea came out on a soft breathless whisper, evolving into a sigh of relief as his hand fell from the switch. Instead, he turned her to him with both hands resting on her shoulders and, with the tip of one finger, he tipped her chin up to him.

"I promise we'll go slow."

"I know." She trusted him, and that single thought caught her off-guard. Yet, right now, she did. She trusted Cade Harper implicitly.

His mouth curved into an impish grin as he stared at her with undisguised desire. "I want you, Taylor. I want to be inside you, feel you around me, holding me."

Lordy! Taylor's gaze slewed to the floor.

"No, don't look away. I need to see your eyes, read them and see what you're feeling. Sex isn't *just* touch and feel or sensory. It's being able to see what the other is thinking, being guided by them. Will you guide me, Taylor?"

"But you're the teacher."

"Am I? Right now, I feel as if I know nothing. That you're teaching me."

His mouth covered hers.

Taylor didn't know what sex would be like. Oh, she'd imagined it. Hours when she'd lain awake at night, making dream-filled love with a faceless lover.

But this?

Cade's touch far outweighed her imaginings, the fumblings of teenage years. Those had been girlish dreams. *And the sweet and innocent kisses from...?*

No, not even Rob's foreplay had ever brought this much pleasure. Pleasure that, deep down, she felt guilty feeling, or enjoying.

Cade's kisses covered her mouth, her eyelids, her jaw, the tip of his tongue twirling the erotic curve of her ear, teeth grazing her earlobe, hands threading through her hair. His kisses sent her head spinning and fired every cell. Seeing the depth of Cade's desire for her fuelled her confidence.

"That's right, sweetheart. You're hot." Cade flicked the clasp on her bra, and her breasts, heavy with need, aching for his touch, fell from their miniscule lacy cloak into his hands.

It felt so very good. So hot. Every sensation escalating. He pulled her closer, her hips connecting with his, his arousal potent, teasing.

Cade was pure temptation in a hundred percent sexy package.

She dropped a hand from around his neck and found what she was looking for. She brushed the head of his penis through his jeans.

Cade sucked back a breath.

She smiled. "You like?"

"You want an answer? I can barely think."

He walked her backward to the bed, then lowered her down. But he didn't follow. Instead, he stood there, his breathing coming in shallow puffs, hands poised on his hips as if he was some swashbuckling pirate about to plunder his captive. He just looked so damned gorgeous.

"Do you always wear such sexy underwear?" he asked.

"Why do you want to know?"

"The outside is prim and proper. The inside is definitely a treat."

"No one knows what I wear beneath my suits. It's my secret."

"Not anymore," he drawled. The tip of his tongue wiped his bottom lip, a slow and provocative action. "Every time I see you, I'll know what you're wearing underneath. Imagine it covering your breasts, wondering if you've a thong or panties on."

"And the garter?" she teased.

"That's a bonus. Garter and stockings, along with lace and silky underwear, can turn a man to jelly."

"How about you? Are you jelly?"

"Not all of me," he said. "So you always wear them?"

"Always." And she smiled up at him, winking.

"Pleased to hear it." He stepped between her legs, edging them wider, and knelt.

Swirls of heat coiled in her center, every fiber aware of him, tensing, wanting his touch.

He didn't disappoint and lightly trailed the back of his hand along her inner thigh.

A rippling sigh escaped Taylor's parted lips. "This is heaven."

"Honey, we haven't even started yet." Leaning forward, he blew a soft funnel of warm, tickling breath along her thigh.

Taylor tensed. Cade's gaze was directed at her very center.

Oh, dear heaven.

And it was. This was heaven and even hell, all joined into one pulsating, sensual moment. A moment when she wanted it all, but wasn't sure she could take much more pleasure.

Her nipples hardened with an aching want. Then he touched her—there—and a sudden shyness took over. She reached down to cover herself, but Cade clasped her hand in his.

"Don't."

Her lips parted, but no sound came. Besides, what did she want to say? She couldn't remember a word.

"You're beautiful. Everywhere."

Taylor's eyes fluttered closed, then jerked open as Cade began a teasing caress, urging her higher, to a need so great she felt she would explode.

This was a different world, a world of heightened sensory exploration. Cade began a gentle quest, brushing from her wet center across her clitoris and back. Over and over.

"I can't... No more," she whispered as her belly clenched and the need for release coiled ever tighter.

"Yes, baby, more. Until you come for me. Let it go."

She squeezed her eyes shut. Tighter. Tighter. Then his fingers entered her, slicked by her wetness. It tipped Taylor over the edge, the sound of him sliding in and out, his thumb brushing over her nub, sending her into paroxysms of pleasure.

"More. I want more," she demanded. In some fantasy world, Taylor was aware of the soft pleading in her voice. It matched exactly how she felt inside, immediate and compelling. But it was what Cade did to her that she centered on. She willed him to bring her to an unknown end.

"Told you so." He leant down and blew a soft draught right onto her center.

"Cade!" She screamed his name, and he repeated the teasing action.

Taylor couldn't hold back. Her body arched as her orgasm flowed to Cade's teasing fingers. Ecstasy coursed through every part of her as her body tensed one last, momentous time, and she fell back, lost in a new and wonderful world.

"Taylor?" Cade bent down and kissed her core, eliciting another violent shudder. Her muscles contracted.

Her eyes fluttered open. "No more. I can't." She didn't think she could survive any more. "That was..." How could she describe what he'd done to her? She tried. "It was beautiful, wonderful, oh wow." A ripple of laughter burst from her lips.

Cade smiled as he pulled himself upright. "Glad you liked it. It's just the beginning." He dropped his hands to his belt buckle and, in what must have been record time, removed his jeans.

Taylor watched him every delicious second, marveling at his strong legs, the muscular thighs that had held her captive by the car. Her gaze traveled his length, wondering what he would taste like, with skin so different in texture from hers. She licked her lips. She wanted to find out.

He was big. Huge.

Her eyes widened as he kicked off his boxer shorts. His erection stood proud. Ready. Her tongue slid over dry lips, palms suddenly sweaty while butterflies revved up in her belly.

Her thighs clenched in natural anticipation.

Easing his powerful frame onto the bed, he took her in his arms—and kissed her.

"Wait." Taylor pulled back and put a hand on his warm chest.

Cade's brow creased, and a glistening bead of sweat trickled down the side of his forehead. She wanted to lick it, but resisted.

"You think I can wait much more, baby?"

"I want to touch you."

"I'll go over the edge."

"Just once," she said, surprised at her own temerity.

"That's all it will take." But Cade acquiesced and lay back, hands hooked beneath his head, watching her every move.

Suddenly, Taylor wasn't so sure.

"You don't have to do this," he said, offering her a way out.

Oh, yes, she did. "It's my turn. Fair's fair."

"Sweetheart, I don't think anything is fair here. You've got me so wound up, I'm ready to explode."

Biting her bottom lip, Taylor tentatively reached for him. She held his penis in her hand, felt his hardness, the ribbed veins engorged with blood and the slick sheen at its tip. She brushed the tip with the pad of her thumb, eliciting a violent shudder through Cade. He squeezed his eyes shut and stiffened, obviously struggling for control. Taylor grinned. It was nice to see she could affect him. "Poor baby," she purred, caressing his length.

"No more words. Time for action." Cade's broad hands spanned her hips, and he rolled her onto her back, his body lining her length. She cradled him between her parted legs, reveling in his hardness, so close to her.

But she wanted him much closer.

His mouth covered a sensitive bud and he sucked, tongue swirling in circles across the nipple before he moved to the other breast.

Taylor let out a deep and contented sigh. This was definitely heaven.

While Cade tended her body, doing deliciously enticing things, she took her pleasure of him, her hands traveling their own path down his back, feeling his muscles beneath her fingertips, his buttocks, cupping his testicles.

Cade groaned and pulled back a fraction. He reached to the bedside table and grabbed the box of condoms. She hadn't even noticed him putting them there. So much for protection. She'd been too busy watching him undress, too hot with wanting to think about safety. Where were her brains?

Expertly, Cade sheathed himself, looked into her eyes and held her gaze. "Thank you."

Taylor frowned, confused by his words. "For what?"

"This is a great honor, Taylor," he said. Then he was inside her. Slow—inch by long, hard inch of him. He kissed her, taking her gasp with his beautiful mouth as he pushed farther, breaking past nature's barrier, stilling momentarily, desire-filled eyes asking a silent question.

"Go on. Please don't stop, Cade."

He filled her to the hilt. All of him. Hard. Powerful—and totally wonderful.

His breathing a staccato rasp, he increased their rhythm. Taylor held onto him, legs wrapped around his hips.

She couldn't think. Could only feel. Feel him inside her, so gloriously deep.

A drawn out sound echoed around them. Her pleasure.

"That's it, sweetheart, go with me," Cade breathed into her ear. His lips found her breast again, sucking, taking her to places she never knew existed, until time meant nothing and she spiraled over the precipice, shuddering her release with Cade holding her tightly, kissing her with a fierce need as he exploded into her.

Chapter Nine

A soporific lethargy inched its way through Taylor as the first rays of daybreak slipped over the horizon and into Cade's bedroom.

Her eyes fluttered open, and a hazy, all-is-well-with-the-world sort of smile curved the corners of her mouth. She snuggled up to Cade, reveling in his closeness, the feel of his warm body wrapped so intimately with hers.

She lay in his arms as finally the overdose of pleasure took its toll and, exhausted, she'd fallen asleep. Now, facing the beginnings of a brand new day, one hand tucked under her head, the other holding Cade's big strong hand in hers, she watched him sleep. Even in sleep, he cupped her breasts. They were still tender.

Too much loving, she purred silently.

No, never too much loving. Last night, Cade had teased every part of her awake, filled her with a want she had no way of controlling.

And this morning, as she listened to his gentle and regular breathing, she wriggled closer, enjoying the erotic sensation his bare skin against hers offered.

Little wonder that, after their action-filled night, she'd lost count sometime after her third orgasm.

Orgasm. Even the word sounded exotic and pleasure-filled.

And so it was. Cade had given her so much pleasure.

Just thinking about it sent a tingle of shivery heat to that very part of her he'd treated with such reverence. With his fingers, his tongue, himself.

So what now?

Taylor jolted at the thought. Cade's hold on her tightened and his beautiful mouth nuzzled at her neck, eliciting a fresh wave of goose bumps down her spine. Closing her eyes, she tried to hold on to every fragment of this moment. His touches, the feelings that threatened to overpower her and send her over the edge with wanting. Knowing that even in sleep Cade desired her, his arousal blatantly announcing the effect she had on him.

Taylor smiled. She didn't want to have to think about reality. This dream, their fantasy, was far better to wake up to.

But the dream was over.

She'd said *once*. And once, well, that was gone. Now what? What did she want? She didn't know the answer to that. Didn't trust herself to think about it. Besides, didn't trusting herself have a way of distorting reality? Guilt was an insidious thing, never leaving her alone.

Not wanting to wake Cade, she unlaced her fingers from his and moved his other hand from her breast. He let out a snuffled snore. Taylor stilled, her breath halting in her throat as she looked at her dark knight. He seemed so at peace. So sexy.

His long, dark lashes fanned angled cheeks, the brush of stubble across his chin only adding to his devilish charm.

He rolled to lie on his stomach, and the sheet covering them slipped, baring his powerful frame, wide shoulders and narrowed hips.

Taylor remembered how she'd cupped them, forcing him closer to her, deeper.

Shifting her gaze, she slipped from the bed and gathered up the closest piece of clothing: Cade's T-shirt. She pulled it over her head. The hem of it came halfway down her thighs, but it felt cozy, even familiar. She dropped her chin toward the fabric, inhaling his scent, a heady fragrance of spice and cinnamon, evocative of the Orient.

Stealing away, she stumbled her way in the half-light of dawn into the lounge and slunk down on the sofa. She reached for a throw and draped it around her shoulders to keep the early morning chill at bay. She could have stayed in bed with Cade, nestled in his arms, warm from the afterglow of their love making, but that was just it. It wasn't *making love*, but sex.

They'd had sex.

Cade had taught her what she'd wanted to know, and now she could go and live her life. Answer *those* questions.

But just the thought of doing that wrought a sadness so sharp and inexplicably deep it frightened Taylor. She didn't understand it, and confusion lit a fear nearing panic deep down inside her. She *should* go—right now. All she had to do was get dressed, slip out and walk away.

Too hard, Taylor. Far too hard.

Taylor sat huddled beneath the brown blanket his sister called a throw and had informed him, with an air of superior knowledge, was "a rich chocolate" and not simply brown.

Cade hesitated to interrupt her, but he needed her, wanted her beside him, with him.

That his feelings were so intense, so desperate, should have worried him. Instead, he battened down any hint of a conscience or any need to analyze it.

"For someone who's kept me awake most of the night, you look mighty good," he said as he stepped into the room. He came to stand in front of her. She looked up at him, eyes round as saucers. "Those dark circles are my fault. Sorry." He grinned, and she smiled back—a smile that didn't quite reach her eyes. Wary concern skittered across his brain. Something was wrong. "Come back to bed, Taylor."

"It's morning," she said.

Cade's panic escalated. "Not quite. The sun hasn't officially hit the day, so I figure we've got at least another ten minutes. Besides, it's Saturday."

"My busiest day of the week," she countered.

"Do you have a wedding?" He really hoped not.

"No." She shook her head. "It's my only weekend free for three months," she added.

"I'm glad."

Taylor went to speak, but seemed to hesitate, and Cade made an instant decision. He wouldn't let her go. Not yet.

"You surprised me," he said, taking both her hands in his. He pulled her upright and wrapped her in his arms, pleased she came so willingly. Cade uttered a sigh of relief, the panic of only seconds ago lessening by degrees. He leant into her and his cheek grazed along her silken tresses. "You smell good."

"Perfume," she said simply.

He nuzzled at her neck, inhaling her fragrance. "Roses," he murmured against her sweet skin. "Roses—and sex."

Taylor shuddered. Her body pressed against his, and his erection strained for release.

"You're one sexy lady, Taylor."

"Me?"

"Yeah. You can tell what you do to me. Even now." And he guided her right hand to where his arousal was already making itself well and truly known.

He kissed her, slow and lingering, using all his skill to woo her back to him. He could tell she was skittery, ready to bolt. Yet in his arms, she had come alive, and the prim young woman who'd walked into his bar a few nights ago had dissolved.

"I know this is scary. I can see it in your eyes, the way they twitch and dart around."

Her blue eyes widened, lightening to the color of a field of summer cornflowers.

He kissed one eyelid, then the other. "See, like right now. You want to take off. Yet you haven't. You're still here, so it's definitely time to go back to bed. I want you to stay. I know we said only once, but right now that doesn't seem nearly enough."

"I should be going," she said.

He kissed her again, then brushing aside the heavy curtain of her hair he trailed butterfly-soft kisses up the enticing curve of her neck. "Later, hmm. Right now, I have other plans for us."

"Plans?" Her question came out a croak.

"Like this." He cupped her bottom through the warmth of the throw, lifting her slightly. She moved with ease, and he smiled. Her legs hooked around his hips, holding on fast.

With Taylor cradled in his arms, Cade turned toward the bedroom. "By the way, did I tell you how sexy you look in my T-shirt?"

She pulled back and looked at him through heavy-lidded eyes. "Better than my underwear?"

A chuckle leapt from deep down in Cade's belly. "Nothing,

sweetheart, is better than those sexy bits of fluff. You can turn me on with hose any time." He kicked the bedroom door open, anticipation roaring through every part of him.

"And the stockings?" she asked as he sat back on the bed and brought her with him. Her sex rubbed against him, a warm invitation he intended to reply to.

"As long as I get to take them off." Cade lifted her slightly then pulled her down in one fluid movement onto his throbbing erection. "Once is definitely not enough."

"Tell me something about you," Taylor asked as she lay replete in Cade's arms hours later. She'd lost count of how many times they'd made love—and it was making love. This wasn't just sex. Sex was emotionless, and what happened between her and Cade was full to the brim with emotion.

Cade lay on his back, bare and blatant, for her eyes only. Just looking at him roused a primal urge in her. His breathing had slowed, but his eyes glittered with unrestrained desire, narrowed and dangerous. Tiny shivers fluttered across her skin, like effervescent bubbles.

"What do you want to know?"

With the tip of her finger, Taylor drew ever-increasing circles on Cade's flat abdomen. "How about something you've never told anyone," she suggested.

His brow furrowed. "That deep?"

"Think of it as getting to know you. A sort of speed dating."

"I think we're past the first date, don't you?" Cade said, cocking his head to one side, his steady gaze holding hers.

She hesitated a fraction, and Cade thought he witnessed a wariness in her eyes. Then it was gone and she spoke. "True.

How about I go first?"

"Thought you'd never offer."

Taylor play punched him on the arm.

"Okay, so what it is it? Are you a closet bungee jumper?"

"No."

"I know, you're afraid of heights."

"That would be good. Imagine trying to put up miles of silk ribbon and afraid to go past the first rung on the ladder. Nope. You'll have to try harder, Cade."

Seconds passed, and slowly, Cade's mouth spread into a devilish grin. "I know." He edged closer. "You're ticklish." He lunged for her. Taylor scrambled but not fast enough before Cade grabbed her, his fingers tickling wherever they touched.

It was heaven and hell mixed together. "No, no. Wrong," Taylor screamed, laughing and almost crying at the same time.

"Yeah, right." Cade pulled back, breathless, his face flushed with humor.

Taylor kept her distance and tried to remain serious. "Am not," she retorted. "I...I have...um...two left feet," she said, scrambling for anything—anything but owning up to tickles.

"I don't believe it. You're a wedding planner."

Taylor shrugged. "Sorry, but that doesn't mean I have to dance. I organize others to do it, that's all."

He laughed—a real belly laugh, and his face lit up, the creases on either side of his mouth dimpling, making Taylor's heart constrict.

"So how do you make sure they can dance if you can't?"

"I tell them to go to dance lessons," she said matter-of-factly. "Right, that's me, now what about you? You can't be good at everything. Oh, I know what it is. You wear shoe lifts. That's it."

"Yeah, right. Not," Cade responded as if insulted, which of course he would be. The man towered over most. He didn't need enhancements.

He's perfect.

Taylor caught herself up sharply with that thought. *Steady on, Sullivan. It's a game, remember?*

But Cade's smile had evaporated, and a deathly silence pervaded the bedroom with each passing second. Taylor reached out, her fingers grazing across his bare arm. "It's okay, you don't have to spill the beans. It's a silly game anyway," she admonished herself, annoyed that she'd started the stupid game anyway, ruining the moment.

"Can't say I run from a challenge."

Taylor brightened. "True."

Cade sucked in a lungful of air, his grip tightening on her fractionally. She pressed herself against him, silently willing him to share. Something of Cade himself—more than sex. That she needed it surprised Taylor—and scared her. When had things changed—from sex to wanting, needing more of Cade than he offered?

"When I was ten, my mother left."

For a moment, Taylor was unsure how to respond. She'd expected fun, fly-on-the-wall humor, not something so traumatic. Finally, she garnered her courage, not knowing if her words would suffice. "I'm so sorry, Cade. That must have been very hard."

"Yeah, well, it's a long time ago. Probably for the best."

"But you didn't think so then?"

"No, not then. My parents argued—a lot. It began from the time they got up until they went to bed. Eventually, Dad came home later and later, but the moment he did, he would get an earful. This wasn't right. That wasn't done. There wasn't enough money. On and on."

"Parents don't realize how much kids take in."

"You can say that again," Cade agreed. His face had taken on a pained expression, eyes dark and sad as if he'd traveled back to his childhood.

"I took it in. Thankfully, Zane doesn't remember much, and Katie was too young to know anything except where the next feed was coming from. Then it stopped."

"Just like that?"

"Yeah, just like that. Mum left. Walked out and everything went silent. Then my father lost it. He couldn't cope with losing her. Oh, he wailed and railed against her, cursing her to the demons, but at night, when he thought we were asleep, he cried."

"Oh..." What could she say? Words seemed inadequate. Taylor's heart bled for Cade, for his family and most of all for his lost childhood. She might have a straight-laced family and be the odd one out, never really feeling she was as good or successful enough for their mold, but she knew deep down they loved her in their own awkward way. They just never said it.

Cade turned over on his side and gathered her in his arms, holding her tightly. "It's hard to admit."

"Why? Because big boys don't cry? That's silly."

He frowned down at her. "No, that's not it. It's because I saw him. Saw him wail into his beer, wallowing in self-pity. No kid wants to see his parent cry."

"No. But it must have been so hard for him."

"Him! What about the kids? About me? I vowed and declared then I wouldn't be like him. Wouldn't let myself be destroyed by..." Cade pulled himself up short and slammed his mouth closed. He spun away from her, but not before she saw the look of sheer horror sprint across his face. He cursed into the dawn.

Taylor wanted to reach out to him, to take away his pain. "It's okay."

"Is it? I've spewed my guts out to you—more than to anyone—ever."

"Thank you."

Brittle laughter fell from his lips. "All this deep stuff, Taylor, isn't me. I don't need it. Not from you. Or anyone."

"But..."

"No buts. Just goes to prove, doesn't it—commitment doesn't work. It's not reliable, and I'm sure as hell not about to trust someone else to make me happy."

It had been an awkward moment, with Cade clearly uncomfortable talking about his past. Instead, Taylor had kissed him.

Kissing solved everything...for the moment.

Kissing Cade. Having sex with Cade. They barely left the bedroom, unless, of course, it was to experiment somewhere else. And sex? Well, sex was something. Sex with Cade, according to Taylor's scale of experience of the power of one, was awesome. Every part of her ached in a tingly, lying-on-a-downy-cloud sort of way.

Just delicious.

The dewy sheen of perspiration cooled against her skin. Cade was watching her, trailing a teasing path up and down her stomach. She purred under his ministrations. "If you keep doing that, I'm not sure how much longer I can hold out."

"That's what I was counting on."

"Really?"

"Sure."

"But we've already..." She counted off on her fingers, eyes widening, and Cade burst into laughter, rolling onto his back and pulling her with him, so that she laid chest-to-chest, hip-to-hip down his length.

"Am I a notch on your bedpost, Ms. Sullivan?"

"Could be," she answered, trying for sophisticated composure and failing miserably as his big, broad hands cupped her buttocks, kneading the flesh, pushing her hips down against his arousal.

"Can you still hold out?"

"Debatable." *Very debatable.*

"Only debatable? I'll have to try harder." He kissed her on the tip of her nose.

"It's the middle of the afternoon," she admonished.

"And your point is?"

"Well...," Taylor prevaricated. "I should go home."

"Do you want to?"

Did she?

"I'll stay."

"Good. I was hoping you'd say that."

Taylor wiped her tongue across her lips. Kiss-swollen lips. Very yummy.

"If you do that again, I'll have to see if your beautiful mouth still tastes as good."

"Oh, believe me, it does. It tastes of you." She brushed the fall of her hair back from her face, knowing the sheet would fall from her breasts. It did, and inside, her tummy did a roll of anticipation.

"You could have been one of those artist's models for Gauguin."

Her eyes widened in mock-horror. "He paints nudes."

Cade's gaze slid down her bare length. "On second thought, cut that idea. I don't fancy a bunch of pervs getting their rocks off looking at you."

"And why not? You're going to spoil a girl's fun."

"So you want a bunch of horny old men staring at you?"

"Ew, maybe not. Anyway, back to us being ensconced in here for hours."

"Ensconced? Big word for this time of the day."

"Exactly. It's 3:30 in the afternoon. Shouldn't you be out mowing the lawn or something?"

"No lawn."

"What about fixing that heap of rust you call cars."

"Rust!" Cade's chest puffed out. "I'll have you know they're classics. Perfection in metal."

"That may be, but it seems to me you've forgotten something. You did promise to show me your etchings."

"Okay."

"Okay? You mean now?"

"Sure. No time like the present." Cade lifted her from him and rolled off the bed. Standing in naked splendor, he simply took Taylor's breath away. He was Adonis. Tanned, muscled and sculpted to perfection.

"Had enough time to get a good look, missy?"

"Oh, God." Taylor yanked the sheet up over her head, every inch of her turning scarlet, even blushing to the roots of her hair. She'd been ogling, all right. How could she not? He was just so darn good to look at.

Cade tugged the sheet back a fraction. "It's okay. It's a compliment, really. I like you looking at me, and what I see in your eyes. Come on." He threw her one of his shirts.

Taylor held it up. "I can't wear this, it's...not decent. I don't have any clean underwear."

Cade winked at her, and she began to blush all over again.

"Cade, you're incorrigible."

"That's me," he said proudly.

Taylor put one arm through the shirtsleeve. "See, it doesn't cover anything."

"Yeah, I know." He wiggled his brows provocatively.

However, Cade did up the buttons, using his closeness to brush his fingertips over her already extended nipples. Then, wrapping an arm around her shoulder, he led her down the stairs from the apartment and through the bar. It was eerily quiet, the sort of unsettling silence that settles over a place which is normally so full of life and laughter. Thankfully, for decency's sake, the bar wasn't opened yet and they were alone.

Out through a side exit, Cade walked in front of her and down a narrow path to an area at the back of the building. The air was late-afternoon cool, and goose bumps dotted her legs and arms. "I'll freeze in just this shirt."

"Don't worry, I know a few ways to keep warm."

"I'm sure you do," she said pettily, though her body heated with the vivid imagery his answer inspired.

Cade gave her a wicked grin. "Glad we're on the same wavelength."

The backyard was dwarfed by a large shed of sorts that spanned its width, with a row of garage roller doors overlooking a cobbled yard. Taylor spied the few tufts of grass struggling to grow between the paving stones.

"And you said you didn't have any lawn," she admonished.

Cade shrugged. "Well, I could always get down on my hands and knees and use nail scissors and manicure it to perfection."

"That I'd like to see."

"Anytime, sweetheart." He brushed her lips with a fleeting kiss.

"Not fair," Taylor whispered.

"Why?"

"Because you only leave me wanting more."

"That's the idea. Tempt and retreat."

Cade drew a key from the pocket of his jeans and proceeded to roll up one of the shed doors to expose beauty in metal.

Taylor could see exactly what he meant. Four cars lined the length of the oversized garage. "Oh, Cade." She stepped close to the Mustang and caressed its curves, but suddenly yanked her hand back and spun to face him. "Is it okay, to touch, I mean?"

"Of course. They're cars. Not museum pieces."

She turned back and walked the length of each one slowly, admiring their silent strength. Each had a gentle beauty about it. The chrome glistened, the paintwork was mirror perfect; all were restored to perfection.

"The Mustang, I know, is a '64, but what year is the pickup?"

"A '48. It's been rodded to go faster. And that one," Cade said pointing to its neighbor, "is a '66 Ford Galaxy. The soft top is a Lincoln Convertible."

"So you're a purist then, an all-Ford man."

"Yeah." He grinned down at her. "Except that the pickup's rodded. You sure know your cars, Taylor. I am impressed."

Taylor walked the line of the cars a second time, hand trailing over each. They were all special in their own right, but in truth the pickup was probably her favorite because it had been the car Cade used for their first date.

First date. How cool did that sound?

"They're beautiful. You've done a good job," she said.

"Thank you."

Cade stood so close that when she turned to face him, their bodies brushed. Heat zinged through every part of her, and his stare was nowhere near any of his cars.

Words failed her. Cade had that effect on her.

He leant forward, forcing her to arch backward, and she came in contact with hard metal. Cade closed in and rested an arm on either side of her.

"That shirt sure looks good on you," he said.

"It's...um too short," she said, tugging at its hem self-consciously.

His gaze lowered to the top of her thighs. "Nope. Definitely the right length. I think you're a bit too done up," he said, flicking one button open. The shirt sides parted, outlining the full curve of her very aroused breasts. Her heart raced a frantic beat, and blood pounded in her veins so hard she was sure she could hear its journey.

Cade pulled back a fraction, eyeing her with a teasing glint in his desire-filled eyes. "Nope. Definitely still too uptight." He flicked another button, and another.

Taylor's breath hung in suspension, lips suddenly dry as any desert as Cade parted her shirtfront. His gaze flared.

"So beautiful," he murmured. Then his mouth was on one

nipple, sucking, teasing her as the curl of his tongue flicked the hard bud repeatedly.

"Cade?"

"Mm, baby, you taste good, just as I remember," he said, leaving one pleasured bud for the other.

Taylor was in heaven and squeezed her eyes shut, blocking out the world, wanting only to feel his touch. His hands lifted her easily, jolting her suddenly alert.

"What are you doing?"

"Don't want to show the world," he rasped against her ear. He yanked the rear door of the Galaxy open. It was made for loving. Intimate. Private. The door closed behind them and, except for the thud of her heart as it hammered, the world went quiet.

Reclining across the back seat, Cade pulled her onto his lap. She went readily, feeling his erection pulse against her.

"Much better," he said and began dotting kisses across her eyes, her face and finally her lips.

Things couldn't be any better. A soft sigh escaped Taylor, and she gave in to the pleasure of it all.

Cade kissing her.

Cade loving her.

Absolutely perfect.

"Cade, where are you?"

Zane! Here.

Cade's hands stilled their journey across her breasts, and he uttered a few choice curses. "Damn, why now?" He looked into Taylor's eyes, silencing her question. "It's my brother." He put a finger against her well-kissed lips and lifted her from him. He turned away and slid toward the door, glancing back at her as he stepped out. "I'll get rid of him."

Taylor curled into the corner of the car, buttoning up Cade's shirt with shaking fingers. Holding her breath, she clutched her hands to her chest. Her heartbeat was frantic, pounding as if her heart were going to explode.

Fancy being caught in the backseat of a car, of all places. What was wrong with her? She wasn't some schoolgirl—okay, so she was still relatively inexperienced, but the back seat—what was she thinking?

Nothing.

Ain't that the truth. Thinking had flown out the window the moment he'd touched her.

Sneaking across the seat, making sure she kept her head below the window line, Taylor listened to the brothers.

"What do you want, Zane?"

"Just dropping off these car parts from Harry Fontain."

"Thanks, now goodbye."

"What? No time for your brother?"

"Nope," Cade bit out harshly.

"None?"

"That's right."

Taylor slid a fraction higher on the seat. Dressed only in his jeans, shoulders broad and flexed, Cade stood with his back to her. But that wasn't the only thing he wore. Scored across his beautiful back were other marks. Scratches. Ones she'd inflicted in the heat of passion when Cade loved her.

Heat scorched her cheeks as she eyed the red love-marks. She remembered the delicious pleasure he'd given her at that moment.

Bad girl!

It seemed, however, Zane wasn't about to budge, and Taylor realized he knew exactly what was going on, because his gaze kept sliding over Cade's shoulder toward the car.

Good Lord, she'd been caught bonking in the back seat. What was she, a tart?

"Go home to your dog, Zane. I'm sure I can hear it barking."

"Tetchy, aren't we?"

"Busy," Cade shot back.

"Yeah, I can see." Zane chuckled. He turned to leave and walked a few feet away. "See ya later, brother. Oh, and bye, Taylor."

Hell and damnation. Zane winked in her direction and gave a final wave goodbye.

Cade wrenched open the car door. "Damn. You okay?"

"No, I'm not." She wrapped her arms across her chest, which was a big mistake as it only emphasized the state of her very sensitive nipples and the reason for their state of grace. "I've got to get out of here and go home. Just like Zane and his dog," she bit out as she scampered out of the car.

"Taylor?"

She brushed him off with a dismissive wave. "No, Cade. Forget it. I can't do this."

She should have listened to her inner warnings, but no, she thought she knew best, knew everything. Wrong! Dumb broad. She was *so* wrong.

Chapter Ten

The pungent aroma of percolating coffee permeated the entire apartment as Taylor showered. Cade had promised her a meal fit for a princess, but right now she wasn't sure she could eat a thing.

Trouble was, she couldn't stay hidden in the bathroom any longer. And the reality was that the fantasy was over.

Switching off the pulsing jet of hot spray, she exited the shower and towelled herself dry. As the fine damp mist evaporated and the mirror cleared, Taylor caught sight of herself.

Hints of purple shadowed beneath her eyes, and there was a flush to her cheeks, a twinkling sparkle in her eyes she'd never noticed before.

That's because you've never had sex before.

She traced the path of her lips. They seemed fuller, more sensual.

Well kissed.

She leant forward, taking a closer inventory of her reflection, hands trailing down her body at the same time. That, too, seemed different, or was it her imagination?

No. She didn't think so. It must be true then, she realized with a satisfied smile. She did feel different. Womanly.

Well loved.

Her breasts felt heavy and full and, as her hand lowered across her flat abdomen, her insides clenched, muscles tensing. She remembered with vivid clarity the feel of Cade inside her. Pulsating. Pleasuring.

Gathering up her clothes, Taylor eyed her dress and grimaced. She hadn't been home since Friday, and the dress looked the worse for wear. But then, she'd barely worn anything all weekend. Simply skin. And it had been wonderful.

She smoothed the wrinkles of her dress and made quick work of her hair, tying it up in a ponytail. She reached for her lip gloss from her handbag and uncapped it. About to glide the pinky stick across her lips, her hand stilled.

She didn't need it. Her lips looked sensational.

Cade had done this.

She capped the lip gloss and tossed it into her bag and dragged in a steadying breath. She exited the bathroom and followed the coffee aroma to the kitchen.

With a tea towel tucked into the waistband of his jeans, Cade busied himself preparing the gourmet delight he'd promised.

"Be ready in a moment."

"Take all the time you need." Taylor enjoyed the show, even finding herself licking her lips. Cade was one delicious man. Everything about him set her senses in a spin. Yet, there was a part of her that held back.

The guilty part.

The part that said, *Watch out, don't trust. You've made this mistake before, and look what happened.*

He placed a pile of pancakes and bacon on the counter. "There you are. Coffee?"

Taylor eyed the food, and her stomach gurgled.

"Anyone would think I've been starving you." He chuckled. "Tuck in."

Finally, she had to ask. "Is it always so awkward the morning after?"

With precise movements, Cade placed his cup on the bench. He gave her an impish shrug. "I wouldn't know."

"But you..."

"The fact is, Taylor, I don't stay. Nor do the women I've been with."

Taylor frowned, her brain wading through Cade's disclosure.

"Besides," he continued, "this isn't quite the morning after, is it? It's Sunday, remember? You arrived Friday night...and stayed."

"And whose fault is that?"

"I kinda think it's both of ours, don't you?"

And what a two days it had been. She'd learnt more about her body and its pleasure capacity in this short time than in her whole life.

You've had a good teacher.

Realizing Cade watched her intently, she lowered her gaze and began to eat.

But there was trouble in paradise. Cade's gourmet endeavors might have been delicious, but she knew she'd no more be able to eat than chew a piece of cardboard. Finally, she put down her knife and fork. She looked at Cade, wishing she didn't have to say what she did. "I really have to go."

"I know."

Disappointment instant, Taylor mentally kicked herself. What had she expected—that he would plead and beg her to stay?

But Cade said no more. Instead, he carried on eating. Taylor watched him as he chewed a piece of bacon, the way his jaw moved, the play of his muscles in his throat, the slide of his tongue over his mouth.

Fantasy versus reality. And sadly, reality tasted sour.

"Sunday's come too quick," he finally said.

Taylor gulped her coffee, ignoring the burn of the scalding liquid as it slid down her throat. She placed the cup on the table, aware her hand was shaking. "Our high noon," she said and linked her fingers together, hiding them beneath the table.

"Something like that," Cade agreed. "So what now?"

Taylor lifted her chin and looked at Cade, stiffening her spine. "Now we go back to our normal lives."

Huh? Who was she kidding? Nothing would ever be normal after this. How could it? Cade had changed her forever.

But she had to pretend it would and so ate the remainder of her meal in silence, all the while battling the urge to plead with Cade to let her stay. Yet, she couldn't. That wasn't part of the bargain. And she always kept her side of a bargain.

The meal over, Taylor was grateful Cade had given her some space. In the bedroom, she retrieved her bag and stood at the edge of the room.

How could one small room have so many memories?

Cade loving her. Teaching her. Tempting her.

Oh, God. This was hard.

"Life is hard," Taylor heard her grandmother say. *"We live, we love and we die."*

Die. Rob had died. And died believing a lie. She'd lied to him and to herself. The sudden, salty sting of tears burned Taylor's eyes. She squeezed them closed.

Time to go.

Bag in hand, she returned to the lounge, hearing the phone ring in the background and Cade's laughing voice as he took the call. "Yeah, nearly all finished here. The plan is working." He covered the mouthpiece as she entered the room. "Hang on a sec." He turned to her. "Can you grab my diary from downstairs? It's in the office, on the desk, a big bulky black affair," he said.

Not really wanting to play the interloper to his phone call, she nodded and headed to the stairs that would take her to the back of the bar.

She walked straight to the desk and saw the large black diary exactly where Cade said it would be.

As she turned to go, she halted and turned full circle, taking in everything about this tiny room. How could it be only a few days since she'd entered this room with her way out proposition? It seemed a lifetime ago. Certainly life-changing, she mused as she hugged the diary to her chest and headed back upstairs.

"Got it." She held it out.

Busy writing something down on a note pad, Cade indicated with a shake of his head that she put it on the bench. "Open it at today's date."

Taylor flipped the pages and trailed her finger down the dates—then froze.

"It can't be."

"Taylor?"

Taylor's legs wobbled, waves of bile rising from her belly to her throat and souring her mouth. The world suddenly went all haywire, a miasmic haze floating in front of her eyes. She struggled to concentrate, shaking her head to purge her brain of the fog as she fumbled for the chair behind her, sinking into its cushioned embrace.

She slammed a hand against her forehead and groaned aloud. "It can't be? How could I have forgotten?"

"Taylor, what's wrong?"

Staring at the black ink in the diary, an accusing blur against the pristine white pages scattered across each date, she trailed a finger once again down the page as if it would erase what she already knew to be inevitable. For one mind-numbing minute, her vision blurred. She blinked repeatedly and wished wholeheartedly that this moment would disappear. But the gods weren't on her side.

She glanced up at Cade. He'd dropped the phone on the bench, though she didn't remember him terminating his call. Tears welled behind her eyes. She willed them away, but nothing was on her side right now and a single tear slid down her cheek.

"Sweetheart?" Cade crouched in front of her, concern creasing his brow. He reached out to wipe her tear, but she jerked violently backward.

"No. Don't touch me."

"Taylor? What's wrong?" he repeated.

"Nothing. Everything. This." She pointed to the diary.

"My diary. What's that got to do with you being upset?"

"Everything." Taylor's shoulders slumped, and a wave of dejection and tiredness overtook her.

And guilt. Don't forget guilt.

"I should have listened."

"Listened to who? You're not making sense."

"To me, Cade. To my conscience."

"What the hell do you mean?"

"I've betrayed someone."

"Betrayed?" Clearly confused, Cade drew a hand through his damp hair and stood. "Taylor, I'm sorry, honey, but you're really not making any sense."

"Don't call me honey. I'm not your *honey*. That sort of endearment is for a couple, people who have a relationship. We don't. And remember, we don't want one, either. Neither of us does," she spat out.

Grim faced, he stared down at her. She wished he wouldn't. Those dark eyes penetrated into her soul. And that was a closed off place.

"I wasn't asking for commitment," he said gently. "What happened, Taylor? Only an hour ago you were inviting me to be with you."

"I looked at your diary, that's what. Today is the tenth of May."

"So?"

"Four years ago today, it would have been my wedding day."

Cade's eyes bugged out, and if it hadn't been so sad and serious, and if she hadn't been wallowing in guilt, Taylor would have laughed. But laughing wasn't even on her radar at the moment.

"It didn't happen. My fiancé died."

Cade moved toward her.

"Don't touch me."

He dropped his hands to his sides, and she hugged her arms tightly around her in a protective band. "I don't need your sympathy."

"So what do you need?"

"I need you to let me go."

Cade stood back, hands in the air. "I'm not stopping you."

For the third night in a row, Cade paced the length of the bar, grateful the staff had disappeared for the day and that his few well-placed scowls had deflected any kindly interrogation from Katie.

Harry Fontain phoned, urging him to join the gang at the footie game.

"Come on, do you good to get out and socialize."

"Forget it. I'm not in the mood."

"So what's up? Women problems?"

"None of your business."

"Ah, so it was the blonde? Didn't think she was your type. Bit too much starch, if you get my drift."

Cade got his drift, all right. "Like I said, Harry, none of your business."

"Man, have you got it bad."

Cade's jaw clenched. He wanted to tell the guy to butt out and go to hell, but the fact that Harry was right on the nose irked the hell out of him.

"What you going to do about it, Cade, ol' boy?"

Cade had declined the offer of any advice and the game of football, and now, as the silence engulfed him and he paced the empty bar, he'd never felt so alone. He came to a halt in the middle of the room and turned full circle. The bar was his flagship, so to speak. His pride and joy. He'd worked damned hard to make it, haul his sorry arse out of the quagmire of his background, a childhood where food was scarce and parents didn't give a damn.

He scowled at the emptiness and downed the shot of

tequila he'd been babysitting for the last few minutes. Zane and Katie didn't know the half of it. He may have been only ten when their parents gave up their parental duties, but he'd protected his brother and sister the best he could.

With the chairs stacked up on the tables, silent shadows played across the walls. The jukebox was switched off, and only ghosts from the past screeched. The place felt empty. Sad, almost. He'd never noticed that before. Somehow, Taylor had bridged a gap, and now she wasn't around, that gap yawned as cavernous as the Grand Canyon.

Back at his desk, Cade spied Taylor's business card. For a few indecisive moments, he stared at the phone.

A jagged laugh escaped his lips. He'd done this before. Every day for three days, and here he was again. Waiting. Watching. And hoping?

He picked up the phone and punched in Taylor's number and waited and waited, and for every long, drawn out second of it he held his breath.

He didn't have a clue what he would say.

Finally, the answer phone kicked in. Again. Just as it had last night and the night before. Cade cursed, using every expletive he could drum up as if it would make everything all right. It didn't, and lousy didn't even cover how crappy he felt.

Always the answer phone, damn it. Even when he phoned her office during business hours, either her assistant Nita stonewalled him or the phone switched automatically to the answer phone. Cade slammed the phone down. The frustration was killing him. And it wasn't just because he'd had a hard-on since Sunday.

What would it take to see Taylor?

"Everything set?" Taylor bundled up her emergency bag and deposited it onto the back seat of her car.

"Sure. Isn't it always?" Nita frowned. "Don't worry, Taylor. You're an expert at this wedding stuff."

Taylor couldn't help but worry. Something always went awry. It was the nature of the marriage business.

Just like your marriage that never was.

"Seeing Cade later?" Nita looked at her surreptitiously. Taylor saw the hope in her assistant's friendly eyes.

"No. It was a one night stand, remember?"

"One night that lasted three days."

"Well, we got a bit carried away, that's all."

We? You mean you.

And that was where her guilt escalated. And the hurt. That she'd forgotten her past, forgotten the date. She always went to the cemetery on that particular anniversary, but this time she'd forgotten.

Too busy having sex with Cade, that's why.

Taylor's mouth pursed into a thin, disapproving line. Yep, got that right, and because of it, guilt gouged a brutal path right through her.

Rob. The perfect man for her. The guy who tempered her "enthusiasm", her parents had said. The boy next door, the budding doctor. Perfect for her family.

Taylor slammed the car door closed. Shame she couldn't slam the door closed on her past. Trouble was, her family made sure her past was kept wide open.

"Nice," Nita cooed, still obviously focused on Cade.

And you aren't?

"He's perfect for you."

"Tell that to my parents."

"Taylor, you're twenty-four. When are you going to tell your family to keep their noses out? They've already found one husband for you. Isn't it time you made your own choices?"

"I have."

"You mean your life as a nun who has nothing but work."

"I love my work." Taylor gave her standard reply to Nita's standard prompt.

Her assistant put an arm around her shoulders. It was nearly the straw that broke the proverbial camel's back. "I know you do. But you need Cade."

Taylor bristled. "No, Nita. You're wrong. What I need to do is to get to this wedding. Last weekend was our only break for a while. Engaged couples are coming out of the woodwork." Taylor stepped out of her assistant's embrace. "I know you mean well, but I've got to make my own life."

"Isn't that what I'm saying?"

"Perhaps," she agreed and mentally counted off the list of things she still had to do. "But let me do it my way. I've spent years doing things my parents' way. I'm not a mega brain box like them. I'm creative. They don't understand that."

"They still look down on your success?" Nita's assessment sadly made reality too real.

"To them, this is playing until I get a proper job."

"You mean like playing doctor or something?"

"Yeah." She grimaced. "Something like that." Taylor observed the flicker of worry cross Nita's bright eyes and gave her assistant a reassuring smile. "Don't worry. It's not going to happen. This business is my baby, my life. I'm not giving it up."

"But you're giving up on Cade?

Was she? Had she? Taylor didn't want to think about it,

but in truth she hadn't thought of anything else but Cade, his touch, what he made her feel, everything about him, since Sunday. She was a total wreck, but, with hours of preparation ahead of her, she willed herself to stay calm and strong. Controlled. "I never had him, Nita. It was a business deal. Simple as that. Cade's a businessman. He understood the deal."

"And you're good at business."

"Yes, I am. Once I've given him the plans for his new bar, the deal is over."

"No chance of resuscitating it?" Nita asked, ever hopeful.

Could she? Would she? No, that was impossible. "How do you resuscitate something that never was?"

"Oh, Taylor, you're fooling yourself. It *was*. Believe me. I see it in your eyes every time the phone rings."

Damn it. Nita saw far too much, while Taylor *felt* too much, and right now she needed to escape. "Gotta go," Taylor chimed and, spinning on her heels, she climbed into her jeep, belted up and started the engine in quick succession. She gave Nita a wave. "I have dinner with my family tonight after the wedding."

Nita grimaced. "Fun with the family."

Taylor refused to ponder that particular statement. History reminded her that fun wasn't something in her parents' well-orchestrated and well-pigeonholed lives.

Chapter Eleven

Cade chewed himself out. He should be anywhere but here. Why the heck hang out at a wedding? He wasn't in the market for one.

He slowed the pickup to a crawl along the curve of the bay, halting across from the reception venue. He switched off the ignition, sat back and watched.

Set against an aqua sky and fringed by a row of *pohutukawa* trees, the Victorian mansion refurbished as a wedding venue bordered one end of the bay. It was picture perfect.

The bridal party had finished their photos, but he wasn't interested in the bridal couple, just the wedding planner.

Man, she looked good. For the last half hour, Taylor, minus her sexy high heels, had waded across the golden sand, circling the couple, arranging the bride's dress and flowers to their utmost elegance for the photographer.

Cade scowled. What a waste. Photos that, after a few months, would lie deserted in the drawer and, if the marriage went belly-up, would most likely be torn in two during some angst-ridden wailing. He eyed the couple with derision. They looked happy—for now. But Cade didn't care if others succumbed to the marriage game. Just don't expect him to imitate their nuptial joy.

So what brought you here, Harper?

Taylor—that's what. She'd haunted his days and nights. He'd tried phoning. Tried ignoring the ache, and that was no bloody use either.

"You're desperate," Zane had informed him, pleased as punch. "Making you a snappy so-and-so."

"Get a life, brother."

"I have one. Do you?"

Dead right he did. He was on the way up with a thriving small chain of bars, about to open a more upscale one in the heart of Yuppieville. What else did he need?

Taylor Sullivan.

Cade sank back into the cushioned leather of the pickup, his hands fisting on the steering wheel as his brother's words replayed for the umpteenth time in his brain.

"Cade." His brother chuckled while helping himself to a whiskey after closing time. "Katie told me you were one unhappy dude."

Cade lifted his head from the drawing he'd spent the last hour doodling—T.A.Y.L.O.R. He screwed up the scrap of paper and tossed it at the bin—and missed. Cursing aloud, he gave his brother his best scowl.

"You two ganging up on me again?"

"Someone has to."

On and on his sibling had railed at him. Eventually, Cade tuned out, though one part of him knew that, deep down, his brother and sister cared. They were his *only* family. Zane and Katie were all that mattered. But now, as he waited outside, watching Taylor, he realized they weren't the only ones who mattered. In fact, they'd slipped down the caring, sharing ladder a couple of notches.

If he could just see her again. He didn't have to talk to her, but then at least he would be able to explain—to himself, hopefully—the raw need that came over him, and finally everything would make sense. Seeing Taylor, he prayed, would help him understand what the hell was going on in his head.

And make it go away.

Cade slammed a fist down hard on the steering wheel, hitting the horn by accident, and a sharp, staccato beep rent the air. Several guests twisted to see where the noise had come from.

"Shit."

Cade craned his neck as the crowd slowly hedged toward the reception rooms, laughing, smiling and dusting the sand off their feet. Taylor was the last. With her back to him, she slipped her heels back on. Killer heels that emphasized her long legs. Sexy legs.

Damn. His eyes shuttered momentarily as he fought to control the scorching desire that fuelled every part of him.

He had it *bad*.

She was dressed in a camel-colored suit that hinted at no inch of skin. But he knew her secret. His gaze slid slowly down her length, and his mouth lifted into a tight smile. Was Taylor wearing that sexy underwear? The lace and silk that cupped her full breasts, and the stockings? Oh yeah... The stockings. Cade shifted uncomfortably. Lace-edged that skimmed her creamy thighs. His erection swelled, growing harder with every teasing image stored in his memory. He'd expected Taylor to follow the guests. Instead, she gave the bride and groom a hug. From his position across the road, Cade struggled to hear their conversation, but their friendly banter washed away on the breeze. With the bridal couple turning to go inside, Taylor gathered her bag and came curbside. She scanned the street as if looking for someone.

Cade frowned. Who was she waiting for?

A boyfriend?

No. He didn't like that idea. No, siree. Not one little bit.

Scrambling out of the pickup, he dug his hands deep into his pockets. It was now or never. And never wasn't really an option.

As he strode across the road, his sneakers crunched on the loose gravel, and a trickle of sweat trailed down the side of his head. He'd never felt so like a school kid in his life. Anxious. Awkward.

"Taylor?" His breath caught in his throat, his lungs refused to work as his heart hammered and his body felt more alive than it had ever been before.

This was life. Before was—was nothing compared to this. He wished he could freeze the moment in time because for one infinitesimal second, as Taylor spun around to face him, delight and joy shone in her eyes and spread across every part of her beautiful face. Then it evaporated, disappeared within the flick of an eye. She held her bag in front of her, as if it were a shield against him. He wanted to reach out and hold her, but she was wary, eyes haunted.

"What are you doing here, Cade?"

Yeah, what? He couldn't think of an answer, at least not one that wouldn't get him arrested.

"I'm in the middle of a wedding," she said, looking back over her shoulder at guests who mingled outside.

"Seems like a success, everyone having a good time."

"You need to go."

Desperation whirred inside him. "I keep thinking about you."

Her lips pursed. "You'll get over it. Just hook up with one of those girls that gives you the come-on at the bar," she said, refusing to look at him.

"You sound jealous."

That caught her attention. Her head jackknifed round, and her mouth opened and closed, but she said nothing. Just looked at him with those dark, cerulean eyes that tore at his soul. He was a drowning man.

"Cade, I can't do this."

He played for time. "This what?"

Taylor looked both ways as if she was making sure the coast was clear.

"It's okay. It's just us two," he said, trying to get her to relax. "Unless you've got a boyfriend lurking in the bushes?" He'd asked the question before he'd actually realized it, but knew gut deep he didn't want to know the answer.

Scaredy cat.

Too damn right, he conceded.

"Low blow, Cade."

He should have felt guilty, but didn't. "Yeah, I'm sorry. Actually, no, I'm not. I'm glad. I don't want you to have a boyfriend."

"Then you'll be pleased I don't."

He stepped closer, relieved that she didn't move away. Instantly, her perfume assailed his senses, and his eyes slid closed for a fraction of time, sparking fragrant memories. "I want it to be me."

"Oh."

"Just 'oh'?" He watched her intently, waiting for some hint she was interested. "You still haven't given me an answer. Why can't you do *this*?"

"Because it wasn't what we agreed. And besides, it was a one-off, a you-helping-me and vice versa sort of thing."

"True. But rules are made to be broken. Why can't we make a new agreement?"

"I don't want to."

"So that's it? I'm supposed to up and walk away?"

"Yes," she said, not really looking at him.

Damn it. He didn't want to. Couldn't. "Shit." Used to being chased and not being the chaser, Cade felt like some damned puppet with someone else pulling the strings.

Try harder. Use your charm.

Cade eyed the reception venue. The Victorian spires, the elegant woodwork. His hands fell to his sides and his shoulders slumped. "Show me what you do, Taylor. Your fantasies."

"Pardon?" That she didn't automatically say no fuelled a tangent of hope in him. Taylor wasn't as immune to him as she made out, but then how could a woman who'd whispered such teasing fantasies during love making be immune?

And your immunity?

Cade ignored his subconscious. "Show me what's involved in a wedding."

"But you don't like weddings."

"That doesn't mean I can't admire your skill at planning one."

"This one?"

"Why not?"

Taylor swiveled toward the stately building. "It's nearly over."

"Can I see, please?"

My God, he was begging. He didn't want her to say no and

scrambled to do everything to prolong the inevitable. "I'm glad you wore your hair up," he said, eyeing her sleek chignon.

Taylor's hand went automatically to her hair, smoothing the strands.

"It bares your neck, and I have an indescribable urge to trail my fingers along your skin."

"Oh."

"Then I'd follow that trail very closely with my lips." He smiled, reveling in being with this woman. This had nothing to do with sex. And everything with simply being together.

Cade choked back a groan. Man, he was really losing it.

"Don't." Her voice was so soft he barely heard it, a whisper on the breeze.

"Don't what?" he teased. "Don't stop? Oh, baby, I definitely don't want to stop. Then there are your long legs. Do you know how tempting they are, Taylor? Legs that lead to heaven. Legs you wrap around me, your breasts pushing against me. I can still hear your whispered pleas as you climaxed."

"No."

He stepped closer still until only inches separated them and heard her faltering breathing. Saw the rise and fall of her breasts beneath her suit.

"You said you wanted more, Taylor."

"That was then."

Cade drew back. *Take it easy. Don't frighten her off. Don't screw up.* "So who's the lucky couple?" he asked. "No difficult questions from the bride this time?"

Taylor's eyes darkened, and she stared up at him through impossibly long lashes. The tip of her tongue slid across her bottom lip. Cade watched it every step of the way. He wanted to tangle with it. Taste it.

"You mean sex?" she said.

"Yeah, those questions." And he couldn't help but smile at her. "They're what got us into this, after all."

Taylor's teeth scraped over her bottom lip. "A few," she said.

"And you were okay?"

Her spine stiffened. "If you mean did I answer them, then yes."

"That's good. It's what you wanted, isn't it?"

"Yes, I suppose so."

"Only suppose? I thought that was the whole idea. Get some experience so you could answer the questions. You know, if there's ever one you can't answer, you can always come to me for some...ah...technical advice."

"Not likely."

Cade chuckled at her answer. "Shame. Could be fun," he countered, hoping to remind Taylor of what she was missing. "So are you going to show me?" He held out his hand and willed her to take it. For a second, he thought she would as her gaze dropped to his outstretched hand before traveling up his arm, washing across his face. Her appraisal held him rigid. He imagined he could even hear her thinking it over, sizing him up. Then she stepped back.

Damn it.

"The wedding reception is underway, but we can take a peek from the sidelines," she said, refusing his hand.

Taylor led the way through the side entrance. The moment they entered, Cade watched her relax as she spoke briefly with guests whose accolades for her work were certainly justified.

Laughter and music met them from every corner.

Decorated in peaches and cream, baskets of flowers hung

from the ceiling, all connected with streams of twined green vines. A myriad of twinkling white lights glittered a thousand-fold from the satin-swathed ceilings and walls while standard candelabra adorned with creamy rose scented candles burned brightly and proffered an intoxicating sense of romance.

"It looks as if heaven has descended," Cade said, impressed.

Finally, Taylor smiled. "Thank you. That's what I wanted."

"You've succeeded." He picked a bud rose from the nearest cascading arrangement and tucked it behind her ear, unable to resist the temptation of trailing his fingers down her cheek. A whisper-soft sound fluttered from her lips.

Cade's gaze scanned the room, capturing its beauty and then returning to Taylor. "I can see why creating something this beautiful gives you a great deal of satisfaction."

"It does." She hugged her bag closer. "Life is hard enough these days. Sometimes it's nice to have little bit of fantasy."

As soon as she spoke, Cade saw reality dawn on Taylor's face, and she jerked backward. She dropped her gaze and hid her wary eyes behind the heavy fall of her lashes.

"Don't hide away. Taylor." He reached out and took her hand in his, a hand so slender it was only half the size of his. He threaded his fingers through hers. "Look at me. Please?"

Her eyes opened, wide, fear-filled.

"Don't be afraid."

She bridled. "I'm not."

"Yes, you are."

With heavy lids, she gazed up at him, her lips parted slightly. He could feel the soft fan of her breath against his skin as she leant toward him. He wanted to kiss her. Had dreamed of this moment for days—and long nights.

"Why are you doing this, Cade?"

He went to answer, but there wasn't really any answer. He was reacting on instinct, something he'd never done before. In the past, he'd always thought things through, planned his life. "Since I met you, my head is in a whirl."

"So take some Panadol."

He ignored her cutting remark, instinctively knew she was as scared as he was. "I'm doing things I see other guys do. Love sick guys."

Shit. Had he said that? He wasn't love sick—he wasn't. Absolutely not. Love wasn't an option. And yet, with a sickening dread, he'd woken up to reality. "You're the first thing I think of when I wake up. I haven't slept for days."

"So I'm your nightmare?"

"No, not a nightmare. A fantasy."

"Go get a book, Cade. I don't want to be in your dreams. That wasn't part of the deal."

"Look, I'm sorry if I made you miss your...date with Rob."

Taylor turned from him them, hiding her expression. "I don't want to talk about it. About him."

Damn. He needed to see her face, her eyes, and very definitely her mouth. "Why not? It's in the past. We all have memories, have to live with them. The word *live* here is the deal. *Live*," he reiterated.

"We're *not* talking about Rob. You're in lust, that's all, Cade. It's all in your pants."

"That's not like you, Taylor. Don't be coarse."

She rounded on him, poking one long, polished nail deep into his chest. "That's just it. You don't know what I'm like."

"But I want to."

"No. Forget it. Forget what we did."

"That, sweetheart, was totally unforgettable."

"Shut up. Just shut up. I'm not going to let you use me to assuage your lust."

"Isn't that exactly what you did? What we did together?"

"It was a business arrangement. But you think you can just smile and get that dimple under my skin and I'll fall into your bed."

"Well, you gotta admit it was good." He chuckled, trying for a smidgen of humor.

But Taylor wasn't about to give an inch. "Good. It was..."

"Hot. We were hot together, sweetheart."

A sudden shout from behind caught them both unawares. "Taylor, there you are. I've been looking everywhere for you. I thought you were going to wait outside for me."

Cade's hand dropped away, and Taylor jerked back and hugged her bag across her chest once more. She brushed back an invisible strand of hair and tugged at her skirt and jacket as if to perfect something that was already perfection. She turned to their interloper.

"Edward." Her voice came out a whisper, and she coughed several times, stammering.

Why was Taylor suddenly so nervous? Cade looked at Edward. Stocky, fortyish dressed in khakis and a button-down plaid shirt. Very staid. Very stoic and reliable.

Nothing like a bar owner.

Cade's gaze twisted back to Taylor, but she refused to meet his stare. His blood heated up a notch. A boyfriend? But she'd said no to his boyfriend question.

"You ready?" Whoever Edward was, the guy had barely acknowledged him.

Cade intended to remedy that. He held out his hand. "Hi,

I'm Cade Harper, and you?"

"Not now, Cade. I've got to go," a flustered Taylor interrupted and grabbed Edward by the elbow as if she intended to hurry away, giving him a warning frown.

"Edward Sullivan. Taylor's brother."

"Oh." Cade eyed Taylor and gave her a quirky half smile, then looked back at her brother. "Nice to meet you. I'm her...boyfriend."

Taylor choked off a gurgling fit of words. "He's not. He's in fantasy land."

But already, Cade and Edward were quietly summing up each other.

"Hmm, Taylor's sure good at fantasy. Very inventive," Cade offered, knowing he'd sent the conversation instantly to overdrive.

"Cade," Taylor warned again and squeezed her eyes shut. Her brother's bulged.

Cade was having fun. And besides, the surprise on Edward's face was too good to miss.

"The folks are waiting for us," Edward reminded his sister and glanced down at his watch. "Weekly dinner, you know," he said as if it explained everything. Edward turned to him. "Hey, why don't you come too? A friend of Taylor's and all that," he said, covering up the awkward silence.

Taylor's grip on her brother's arm clearly tightened. "No, he can't."

"Sure I can."

She shifted her narrowed gaze to him, daring him.

Oh, he dared, and he gave her his best beaming smile. He held out a hand to Edward. "Love to come and meet the family. Taylor's told me so much about you all, haven't you, honey?"

"Hon—" Taylor choked over the word, her mouth opening and closing several times.

"Fly catching?" He winked at her.

"Grr..." She shot him a scathing glare.

"Oops, think I'm in trouble."

"You can count on it." Taylor linked her arm with her brother and dragged him, almost running, away, leaving Cade in her wake to watch her cute little butt sashay. "Great view," he called just loud enough so she could hear.

"Oh, you..." She speared him a withering glance over her shoulder.

He gave her a relaxed wave, winked and grinned at the same time. Her lips pursed, and she snapped her head back as a laughter rumbled from his throat. "Yep, the day sure has improved—substantially."

Chapter Twelve

Oh, God. What was wrong with her? Everything Cade said was true. She would have fallen into bed with him. All it would have taken was one of those sexy smiles of his aimed in her direction.

Unadulterated and oh-so-very hot lust held her in its grip. Her body craved his touch. But she couldn't give in to it.

It all came down to that one moment, a slice of history that hung forever between her and life, kept there by those who cared for her, yet who didn't realize the memory was entwined with guilt and remorse.

A memory that wouldn't release her.

"Blast it." Edward kicked at one of the rear tires. "It's shot."

Taylor eyed her brother Edward's vehicle across the carpark. The tire was flat as any pancake. "Change it. The wedding staff has everything in hand. I'm not needed here. I want to leave, now, Edward."

"Can't. The spare's not exactly spare. This is the second flat I've had in a couple of days. The guys at the garage were getting in a specialist tire for me."

"You mean to say we've got to walk?"

"'Course not," Cade chimed in. "There's always the pickup." He thumbed toward his vehicle parked across the road.

Taylor's vision shifted toward the parked vehicle. "No. No way. I'm not getting in your car. Not again."

One dark brow rose, and his mouth quirked to one side. Taylor wanted to slap that smile right off his face, erase it, because it did far too many things to her, things she didn't want.

Liar!

"You didn't seem to mind it last time, if I remember rightly."

Oh, he remembered all right. And she did too.

"First and last time," she reiterated. She tucked her bag under her arm and twisted back to her brother. "We'll walk."

"I can't. Old Achilles injury," her brother chimed in.

"Edward, I'll get you for this. I don't need this right now."

"What she means, Edward, is she doesn't want to ride with me."

"I don't want to be with you anywhere, Cade."

"Could have fooled me."

"Mother's a stickler for punctuality, Taylor," her brother added as fuel for the fire, tapping his watch.

"Ooh." She stamped her foot. "What is it about you men? You always stick together."

"Predisposed survival instinct," Cade offered.

"More like pigheadedness," she shot back, adding the worst glare she could manifest to boot. Taylor glanced at her watch. There was no way out of it. She was due at her parents' for dinner ten minutes ago, and Edward was right: being late for their mother wasn't a good start to what she knew would be an awkward evening.

After climbing into the pickup, Taylor found herself sandwiched between her brother and Cade. She did her best to keep well clear of Mr. Harper, but every time he took a right corner, she was forced ever closer to him, suffering his hard, virile body rubbing against hers.

While her brother and Cade held a chatty banter over her head, she remained silent, doing her best to ignore the hunk. When she caught his easy smile, she jerked away and turned. She wouldn't look.

Damn him. And all men in general. Cade, however, was obviously enjoying every single moment of this.

Of course he would. He got his own way—again.

"Here we are. Home sweet home," Edward announced as he directed Cade up the drive to the family home.

Cade brought the pickup to a halt, and Taylor uttered a grunt as she shoved past him, stumbling over his long legs in the process. She had to get out, get some distance between them. She needed to breathe.

Cade followed, stretching as he eyed her parents' home. "Nice place."

"They've lived here since they married. Bit of a mausoleum though," Edward answered. "Gotta run. The folks are inside." He nodded toward the house.

"You're not staying?" A fresh wave of panic reared its ugly head. She didn't want to go inside. Not alone. And certainly not with Cade in tow. This was worsening by the second.

But her brother ignored her pleas, wheeled his racing bike from the garage and left without a backward glance. Left her—with Cade—and her mother.

"You don't have to come in. You can go," she said to Cade. *Please go.*

"Make an excuse, you mean?"

"Yeah, Edward was just being friendly."

"Nice guy."

She shrugged.

Just then, the screen door opened and her mother came out to the porch. "Taylor?"

"Typical." Taylor didn't know why she hoped for something different. It never happened. Her mother never said it was lovely to see her, ask how she was, simply uttered her name. One word with so much condemnation tied into it.

Taylor's mouth turned down, and she blinked away the sudden threat of tears. "Hi, Mum. Edward suggested I bring Cade."

"I see." Again, not hello. Welcome. Nothing. Instead, her mother linked her fingers, turned on her heel and walked back inside.

Embarrassed by her relation's brutal rudeness, Taylor didn't know what to say.

"She doesn't seem pleased to see me."

"She's like that with everyone."

"Even you, it seems."

Taylor sighed. "Usually."

"And I thought having a drunk for a father and a mother who didn't bother was hard work."

"Don't, Cade. Please don't. Family is, well, family." She shrugged, battling weary resignation. "You get used to it."

With legs heavy as lead, Taylor took the steps with Cade at her side. She couldn't see any way out of this meeting and was determined to get it over with as quickly as possible.

Her parents had loved Rob. They remembered him, made sure, even after his death, he was in her life, always. They made her feel guilty for wanting something else. For being different.

She stepped inside the distinctive villa and waited for Cade's reaction.

He would react. Everyone did. "Your parents sure are into antiques," he said, eyeballing with incredulity the overstuffed room. Taylor followed his gaze. The place was definitely weird. Every nook and cranny had been stuffed to bursting with furniture, plate collections, stuffed animals and Victoriana.

"Try living with it."

"Nightmares?" Cade surmised.

"Frequently," she returned and gave him a lopsided grin.

Her mother turned to face her and Cade. "This is...ah...a friend, Mother. Cade Harper."

Cade held his hand out to her mother, but in true form, her mother looked at Cade as if there were something not quite acceptable. Taylor cringed. *Here it goes again.* Same old, same old.

"Sherry, ah...Mr. Harper?"

"Call me Cade."

Her mother's mouth twitched slightly, as if Cade had said something distasteful. She poured three small glasses of sherry and handed one to Taylor and another to Cade. Seeing the tiny stem in Cade's large hand, delicate versus strong, brought a sudden flurry of tears to Taylor's eyes. She quickly turned and brushed them away. Everything was so up and down. And now this. She knew the outcome. It was always the same.

Cade wasn't Rob.

Just then her parent's housekeeper walked in. Dressed in black with a crisp white apron tied around her waist, hair tied in a severe bun, she announced dinner. "Mr. Sullivan is running late, but dinner is ready, ma'am."

Cade's hand jerked. Droplets of the sherry spilled over the tip of his glass. Taylor caught him staring at her. "A maid?" he mouthed.

Taylor just shrugged. She'd given up trying to explain her parents.

Clearly disapproving, her mother stood and walked to the connecting dining room and sat. Taylor knew she had no choice but to follow, so she did as was expected.

"Your father knows how much I like us to eat together, especially on this occasion."

"Occasion? Is it a birthday?" Cade's question caught Taylor unawares. She should have warned him. She eyed her mother, wishing the woman would forget and let her forget as well.

Here it comes.

"It's Rob's anniversary. Taylor's fiancé," her mother explained.

"Ex-fiancé," Cade corrected.

In slow motion, her mother placed the starched white linen napkin on her lap, smoothing out invisible creases. She ignored Cade's correction. "Rob was such a beautiful and talented young man. He was way ahead of his time, you know."

"With what?"

Taylor cringed. She willed Cade to shut up, to just say sorry, he had to go. Once her mother started…

"Mathematics, of course."

Cade's gaze swiveled in her direction, brows arching in an unspoken question.

"My parents lecture at universities all around the world."

"In mathematics?"

Her mother straightened, her mouth twitching at the corners into an imitation of a smile. "Of course. And Rob would have followed in our footsteps. He was on his way."

"Sounds perfect."

"It was. He was absolutely just the man for our Taylor. He wouldn't have minded her...ah...creative tangents."

"Mother." Dear God. Nothing had changed. Rob was perfect. She *was* to be perfected.

Taylor watched Cade's brows knot. The pulse in the side of his neck throbbed erratically, its beat hypnotizing. She remembered licking it, tasting his skin.

"Tangents?"

"This business of hers. We've always told Taylor she needs to take things seriously, then she'll find her place."

"Place?" The muscles in Cade's neck corded, a disappointed set to his mouth.

This conversation didn't bode well.

"You know her brother has been awarded a fellowship at a prestigious university, and Kiera, her sister, is head surgeon now."

"Impressive."

"Yes." Her mother sighed, gray eyes flickering briefly in her direction.

Cade stood and placed his glass on the mahogany side table. He turned to her mother. "Actually, I think Taylor's business is a great success."

"Perhaps."

"Perhaps nothing, Mrs. Sullivan. Taylor is creative, dedicated and very successful. She gives couples the chance to start life with their dream wedding. Isn't that what it's all about? Dreams of the future?"

For a few tense, silent moments, it was as if there were a standoff between Cade and her mother. In this house, no one challenged her mother, but then her mother had never battled Cade.

Go Cade, she cheered silently.

"What do you do, Mr. Harper?" her mother asked, her imperious gaze never wavering.

"I own a bar."

"Several, actually, Mother," Taylor interrupted. "Plus Cade is opening a new line of boutique bars."

"Really. How interesting." She might have said it, but Taylor knew her mother was looking down her very long nose right now. Cade, in her opinion, wasn't of any interest and more than likely was at the bottom of the pecking order.

"It is, Mrs. Sullivan. The cash flow is great. I own all the buildings. I'm a real successful guy. I didn't go to university, but then, unlike you, I don't judge people by a piece of paper that says whether they studied or not. And, then, of course, I'm not Rob."

"Cade!" His name slipped from her lips in a shocked gasp, but he silenced her with a flick of his hand.

"Rob, Mrs. Sullivan, is dead. Long gone. You can still love a dead man, but they're not much use. Except to you, that is."

"What are you talking about? Where did you find this...?"

"Boor? Is that the word you're trying to find, to pigeonhole me with? Sorry. I might not have fancy manners or come from the right side of the tracks, but what I have is mine. I've worked damned hard for every piece of brick and mortar, and I'm proud of it."

"I...never." Her mother stumbled over her words, something Taylor had never, ever seen.

Go, Cade. Go!

"No, that's right," Cade interrupted her. "You've not lived. You've set yourself up here in your ivory tower with your overstuffed antiques and dead animals hanging on the walls.

You judge everyone by your own limiting standards. Even your daughter."

"Cade, don't."

He turned to her, and she saw the fire in his eyes burning bright. "It's okay, sweetheart. Your mother needs to hear this. It's about time."

Taylor agreed silently. Trouble was, she'd never had the guts.

"You judge Taylor by some oddball idea that she needs to be the same as you and your over qualified highfalutin brain boxes. Well, she might not have a Mensa IQ, but she's bright, she's funny, she's creative and she's making her own way in the world. But you can't let go, can you? You want her to fit into that precise, preconceived world of yours. You want her so-called perfect."

"That's enough." Finally, her mother found her voice. Her face white with fury, her gray eyes narrowed. "Taylor needs—"

"To be Taylor, Mrs. Sullivan. Let her do her own thing."

"That sounds like some psychobabble."

"No. She's just different. From you. From me. She is simply herself. Taylor is herself. And that's more than enough."

Unyielding, her mother pulled herself out of her chair. Taylor could see by her steely expression none of what Cade had said in Taylor's favor had sunk in. Florence Sullivan was too set in her ways, too rigid to understand.

"Rob was a dear family friend."

"I'm not doubting that. He was your great white hope, so to speak. You hoped to use him to whip Taylor into shape. But he's dead. You can't keep using him every year to control your daughter."

"I think, Mr. Harper," her mother said through thinned lips, "you had better go."

Taylor's gaze shifted downward. Her mother had balled the napkin in one fist.

"Come on." Cade grabbed her hand and tugged. "We're out of here."

"Taylor, dinner is served," her mother cut in.

Dark, stormy eyes stared down into her face. Eyes that had burned brightly as he'd taught her, loved her and now released her. Why did she feel she was in a tug of war, with her being the so-called piggy in the middle? Taylor stood and wiped the back of her hand across her forehead. There was a stab of pain behind her eyes. "Another night, Mother. I think I had better go too."

"But Rob's anniversary."

"Cade's right. He's dead. I've got to go." Turning on her heel, she ran from the room, bypassed the row of deer heads that had scared the living daylights out of her as a child. She yanked open the front door and rushed outside, then doubled over, hands resting on her thighs as her chest heaved and she struggled for oxygen.

"Get in."

Taylor lifted her head and peered through strands of hair that had fallen free.

"Taylor. Get in. Now."

Hauling herself upright, she reacted on auto-pilot and slid into the pickup. Before she'd even closed the door, Cade fired the engine and they were down the drive and around the first corner.

"Cade?"

"Don't say a word, Taylor. Not right now."

They came to a steep curve in the road, the narrowed

entrance to Mt. Victoria.

"Why here?"

"I need to calm down. Think. Because believe me, I've never been so furious."

"I'm sorry."

"You should be because it's you I'm angry with."

"Me?"

"Yeah. Why'd you let her do it, Taylor? Why'd you let her stifle you?"

"You didn't have to stick up for me."

"I know that, but how long are you prepared to play second fiddle to a dead man?"

"I..."

Cade brought the car to a halt at the edge of the lookout. It was dark, yet the night sky shone with the reflection of a million city lights bouncing against the inky darkness.

Enveloped by a numbing sadness, Taylor sucked in a steadying breath. "Sometimes it was simply easier. When you've a Mensa IQ brother and sister, as well as your parents, and you're the odd one out, it's easier to think it doesn't matter and not rock the boat."

"But you did rock it. You started your business. That surely wasn't in their plans for you."

"No, it wasn't. After Rob died, they thought I'd just fall back into place again, but his death lit something else in me, a need to do what I wanted to do."

"So you started Creative Weddings."

"Something like that," she agreed.

"Good on you."

A slow smile tilted the corners of Taylor's mouth. "Yeah,

good on me." Tiny at first, a tinkling sound erupted from her throat, then a full, hearty belly rumble brewed down deep, bubbling up until she couldn't hold it back any longer.

"No one has ever spoken to my mother like that."

"Tough. First time for everything."

"That's what got us here in the first place," Taylor said softly.

"Mm." Cade slid over the seat toward her and wrapped her in his arms. "Usually, after the first time, there's a second time."

"I think we've already had that," she countered playfully, hands resting on his chest. She could feel the heat beneath her fingertips, the thrust of his pulse. She swallowed hard.

"Who's counting?" he asked, giving her a cheeky grin.

"Not me."

"I was hoping you'd say that."

"Then what are you waiting for?"

"This." And his mouth claimed hers. Hot. Fast. And furious. Gathered in his arms, Taylor felt as if she'd come home. This was what she had been waiting for. Not just for the last few days, but since forever.

"Delicious," Cade murmured as his mouth moved over hers, hands in her hair. He pulled the pins from her hair. "I've been waiting all afternoon to do this." In seconds, her hair cascaded around her shoulders. He buried his face in the loosened strands. "You smell of violets and roses."

"Very poetic."

"I am, aren't I?" he said, dotting tiny kisses along her eyelids.

Taylor sighed. This was beautiful and arousing. But it wasn't enough. She wanted more. "I want you, Cade. Inside me," she whispered. She nipped his lobe and felt a tremor ripple through him.

"Here?"

"Anywhere." Her hands fumbled with his shirt, pulling it free. She smiled, sliding the tip of her tongue across her lips. His chest heaved. She'd caused that. It felt good. She had power over him. Sweet, delicious, sinful power.

Taylor hadn't realized how exciting sex in a confined space could be. The windows steamed up, and her body zinged with unbridled anticipation.

"My turn, I believe," Cade drawled. He slid the zip on the back of her dress down with infinite ease. "Oh yeah." His breath hung on the air, thick with promise, his gaze roaming over her—*all* over. "I wondered." He leaned forward and kissed her gently at the apex of her breasts, just above the lace bow. Taylor's neck arched back. She gloried in him.

"I'd hoped," he said, gazing at the lacy concoction she wore.

Lifting herself, Taylor slid one leg over Cade. The moment she lowered herself, her sex met his arousal. Clothes might have not existed, the molten heat burgeoning between them explosive.

As her legs spread wide and she balanced against Cade, her dress rose up.

Outside, a soft breeze fluttered around the lone vehicle, and the shriek of an owl pierced the silence.

Taylor shuddered.

"Maybe the ghost of the mountain is with us," Cade said.

Goose bumps slithered up and down her bare skin.

"Hey, I'm here." He took her in his arms, rekindling his kisses, hands cupping her breasts, teasing one nipple between his fingers.

"I want you." A simple statement, full of promise and anticipation. Taylor reached for Cade's zip and slid it down.

He chuckled. "My, how things have changed."

Her hands stilled.

"No, don't stop."

Taylor reached for him, feeling the throbbing power of him in her hand. Her thumb brushed across the tip, and Cade let out a shuddering moan.

"I've created a teaser."

"You taught me well," she responded. "Lift me."

"Your wish is my command." Cade cupped her buttocks, his warm fingers kneading her flesh as he did as he was told. She brought the head of his erection to her center, paused for a moment to sheath him in a condom.

Then he was there. The tip of him brushed against her wetness. She pushed down. Hard. Fast. Taking all of him.

Her muscles gripped him, thighs tightening as best she could, and she rocked. Not gently, but in a frantic race to the finish line. He sucked at her nipples, laving the buds till they ached, and as he moved from one to the other, the cold air hardened them further.

"Not fair, I want to touch you." Taylor gripped his shoulders and leant forward.

"Baby, you already have all of me." He pushed himself deeper.

But Taylor reached down between them, circling the base of his erection with her fingers. She trailed her nails across his skin, felt the force of his shudder rip through him to her as she, too, reached her fantasy: Cade—loving her.

Taylor couldn't speak, overwhelmed by feelings and emotions. She stared down at Cade. Really looked at him. This man had stood up for her, taken her side when no one ever had. He believed in her work, liked it—which was good. Cade cared enough to help her with something so personal, something he'd made so exquisite, she'd never forget it for as long as she lived.

She kissed the tip of his chin. "Thank you for making it special."

"Just doing what a knight in shining armor does," he responded. Then he kissed her back. One long, sweet kiss, full of tenderness and joy and loving.

A heavy, contented sigh slid from her lips.

Her knight. It had a certain ring to it.

"Cade, I..." Taylor slammed her lips closed. She'd nearly said it. Oh, my God. The words were on the tip of her tongue, wrapped right around her heart. Three words. Words that, until that very moment, she hadn't realized were there, or were even a part of her.

She loved Cade Harper.

Really loved him.

How was it possible in just a few days? Did love happen like that? Instantly? Where was the courtship, the slow-to-grow love? This was hot, deep, lustful. Yet it was still real.

She couldn't tell him. Cade didn't believe in love or marriage. He'd said so. And besides, it wasn't part of the bargain they'd made. He'd called himself her boyfriend in front of Edward, but Taylor knew that had simply been a ploy to...well, have sex with her.

What a fool she'd been. She'd done the one thing she said she wouldn't do. She'd fallen for a man who wanted her only for sex, even though that was exactly how she'd wanted it. Just sex.

Cade was the ultimate love 'em and leave 'em kinda guy, not someone who'd stay. But now Taylor didn't want part-time. She wanted a permanent man.

Her admission surprised her. Right up until this very minute, Taylor hadn't believed she wanted anything. She'd never let herself think about it. Well, not really.

Yes, you have. Every time you watch your brides walk down the aisle, you imagine it's you.

Totally bewildered by her raw feelings, she closed her eyes. She didn't want Cade reading her thoughts, seeing into her soul.

Or to scare him off!

"Taylor?"

She shuddered. What was she doing? Half-naked up a mountain with a man who had no use for her—well, only one use, and that would break her heart, eventually.

"I have to get out of here." Yanking herself from Cade's embrace, she skittered across the seat, pulling clothes after her. She wrenched open the door, climbed out into the night and slipped on her dress.

"What are you doing?"

"Exactly what I should have done earlier instead of listening to my hormones. I'm going home."

"You can't walk home at this time of night."

"There's plenty of light."

"Walking down the side of a mountain?"

"A small hill," she corrected.

"Whatever." Cade glanced over the near-vertical drop that wound down the extinct volcano. "You'll break your damned neck."

"Not a problem. That'll let you off the hook."

"What the hell are you talking about, Taylor?"

She shook her head. "Never mind, pass me my purse." She shrugged on her jacket and battled to stop her teeth from chattering at the same time.

"No."

She held out her hand. "Give it to me, Cade."

"Get in. I'll take you home. Bloody women. Never can figure them out."

"You're right, of course. Walking down Mt. Victoria in the dead of night would be foolish. Silly me." She got back in the front seat and closed the door, but kept herself well and truly on the other side of the vehicle.

"Taylor?"

Taylor kept her eyes riveted on the nothingness of the dark night. At the sound of his voice, her skin tingled and the hairs on her arms prickled. Her mouth went dry and she tried to moisten her lips, wiping the tip of her tongue across them.

Dumb move. She could taste him—all over again.

Cade reached for her, but she pushed herself toward the door. "No touching, Cade."

"That's not what you said a minute ago. You wanted me to touch you—everywhere," he said, his voice husky and tainted with the aftermath of sex.

"It's over. We've concluded our business deal. You've the plans you need so you can open the new bar, and I've..."

"Had sex."

Her shocked gasp filled the space between them. "Don't be crass."

"Why not? You've reduced it to that level."

"I...I'm sorry, that wasn't what I meant."

"Then what did you mean? Wham, bam, thank you, Cade?"

"What did you expect? That I'd fall for your charms, stay in bed a bit longer, until *you* decide it's over? Well, no way, that isn't how it's going to be. As of now, our business association is terminated." She squeezed her eyes shut, forcing back the threat of tears.

She loved him. Truly. Deeply. Totally. Yet she would keep that secret to herself. Cade had to figure out what he wanted first, and it couldn't be *just* her body.

Lust *wasn't* love.

He said he needed to see her, that he ached for her. Well, he had to figure out what that ache was.

Chapter Thirteen

"You ditched him? Taylor, are you absolutely nuts?" Nita punched the print key on the keyboard while staring at her above the screen.

Taylor remained mute. Oh, she was nuts all right. Completely bonkers in love with the guy, but she'd still walked away.

Gathering up the printed emails, queries, bookings and replies regarding venues, et cetera, Nita handed them over to Taylor and sank back down on her chair. Her brows knitted. "I don't understand, Taylor. You fancy the pants off the guy, right?"

Yep, she'd done that—more than once. Taylor nodded.

"So why say *sayonara*?"

"Because that was the deal."

"Blah, blah, deal shmeal."

"Look, we've got weddings coming out of our ears. I don't have time to discuss this."

"You should."

Taylor turned and rested her hands on her hips. She gave Nita a disbelieving stare. "Why exactly?"

"Because you're turning into your mother. You're living your life for your past, not for what could be."

Nita's observations were too close for comfort, and Taylor looked away. "Don't be fanciful," she said, trying to counter her assistant's argument, aware of a sense of sinking in a quagmire of denial. "I know we're in the business of making fantasies come true, but that's for other people. Not me."

"And why not?"

"Just *because*, that's all. Now let's get going. I've got to get to the caterers before ten."

Gathering up her bag, Taylor made it quite clear to Nita she didn't want to discuss her love life any further, and thankfully, the young woman took the hint. But the trouble was, although Taylor wasn't verbalizing them, thoughts of Cade wouldn't abate.

She loved him. It was as simple as that. And as complicated.

She had put her life on hold for four years, lived it according to how others decreed. Now she had to do it for herself, and Cade had to decide what he wanted.

Hasn't he already?

No. No. No. He had to decide. Her—or to hold onto *his* past, just as she'd been doing.

But first, Taylor had one more visit to make. A last one. She had to say goodbye to someone.

Home to thousands of souls, all loved, all departed, the gently rolling contours of Schnapper Rock cemetery overlooked the western inlet of the Manukau harbor. It was a world of peace, with the soft caw of gulls flying overhead and the sway of the native trees shifting in the slight breeze.

Everywhere, bouquets, potted plants and single stems

dotted the landscape, every one of them left for someone gone from this world, but remembered by those left behind.

Several narrow paths, just wide enough for a car to traverse, meandered through the park-like grounds. Taylor treaded the path so well remembered across the grass, counting row upon row of gravestones. Tears welled for a life cut down far too early, never having the chance to reach its potential.

So very sad.

Yet Rob had been glad to go and had borne his pain with dignity.

He'd known her secret, though he'd never said a word. Just asked her to be happy.

But being happy had proved to be a momentous task when she'd been riddled with relief that he was gone and she was still alive.

Now Taylor had come to say a final goodbye and to ask for forgiveness.

Bending down in front of the gravestone and seeing his name, the lettering worn by nature, Taylor cried.

For Rob. For herself. For life.

"I've found a man to love, Rob. A good man. Kind, considerate. But he doesn't want to love anyone. He hurts too much, so I've decided to go on, alone, and start living *my* life. You won't be forgotten, but I need to be *me*, not the person my parents wanted to mold me into." Pushing herself up from the cushioning grass, Taylor brushed her hand across the top of the gravestone.

It felt cold. Dead.

"You're going out dressed like that?" Nita's eyes bugged.

"Something wrong?" she asked, trying for nonchalance.

"You are joking, aren't you?"

"Do I look like it?"

Nita shook her head.

Taylor could understand her assistant's bafflement. She patted her hip. "Don't they look good? Is my behind too big?" She giggled, pirouetting full circle.

"Big butt? You've got to be joking, though not much of it is covered."

Taylor squirmed. Nita was dead right. "They're leather."

"I can see that." Nita eyed the shiny black shorts that appeared to be so tight they could have been painted on.

They felt exactly as they looked. Too tight. And definitely very sexy.

"Where on earth did you get biker shorts?"

"We deal in fantasy," Taylor said, giving her a cheeky grin. "So I hired them from a fancy dress shop. The top too," she said, thumbing the leather vest. The brass stud buttons wouldn't do right up and, unfortunately, left very little to the imagination. Taylor viewed her reflection in the full-length mirror. They were jailbait material. "How women can wear these on bikes, I haven't a clue. My butt is blue."

"Sure is cute, though."

"You think?" Taylor twisted again so she could see her rear in the mirror. "Oh, Lordy."

"See what I mean?" Nita chuckled.

She sure did. Butterflies erupted into a tango in her stomach and beads of perspiration broke out on her forehead. "Being a bad girl is hard work. Maybe I shouldn't go."

"Why not? You want to, don't you?"

Taylor nodded. She'd left her long hair loose, and the thick tresses cascaded around her bare arms. As it brushed against her skin, its texture sent a hot shiver up and down her spine.

That's excitement and anticipation, her subconscious chided.

She did want to go. But for what reason? "Cade isn't interested in me. He would have contacted me otherwise." Taylor heard the uncertainty in her voice. Nothing could cancel it out, and she'd been battling it for days.

Yet here she was, ready to roll.

Or fall.

Nita clasped her hand. "The truth is, I don't know, and neither do you. Men are a stubborn breed. Who knows what Cade is thinking?"

"He wanted sex."

"So did you."

"I know. At first, but..." Love had got in the way.

"Oh, my goodness." Nita slapped a hand on her forehead, eyes twinkling with excitement. "I've got it. You've fallen for him, haven't you? You're in love with the hunk."

Wordlessly, Taylor nodded.

"So what are you doing here? Go get him."

Lordy, this was way too hard. "What if he doesn't want me?"

"Oh, he wants you."

"Sex only. I don't want that, Nita. I want more."

"Then make him want more. Teach him to want more."

"Can I do that?"

"Sure you can. Why are you going to the bar? I mean, I presume it's Cade's bar you're going to?"

"What you mean is, why am I going dressed like this?"

"Uh-huh." Nita gave her the once over—again.

"They say a man lusts after what he can't have," Taylor finally conceded.

"And you intend for Mr. Harper to be drooling."

"Got it in one." She smiled.

"Cool. Now would it be a good time to ask for a pay rise?"

Taylor laughed, suddenly excited. Tonight was about her and Cade. She'd made her decision. She wanted to live.

Determination set, she walked to the door.

"You're temptation all wrapped up in one, Taylor."

"You think?" she said, loving for the first time the freedom to fantasize, to let go, even if it was just a little.

"Cade is one lucky guy."

Hand on the doorknob, Taylor halted. "Cade might see something he likes, but until he decides what he *really* wants, then this package isn't part of the deal."

"So go sock it to him, boss. Make him realize what he's missing and what he could lose."

"But does he want it enough? That's the sixty-four million dollar question."

The noise was the same. So, too, the crowd, even the gentle breeze embroidered with the salty tang from the nearby waves. Everything was *exactly* the same.

Except you, Sullivan.

She was different.

She'd made an exciting, thrilling, but scary discovery and fallen in love with a man who actively shied from love.

Tonight, however, she was here to have fun, and if that meant she teased and taunted Cade into a spin, well and good. She wanted him to come to grips with what he could lose—had lost because of fear—unless he dug deep into his past. He needed to deal with it before the future could begin.

"Hey, Taylor, looking for Cade?"

Attacked by a sudden uncertainty, Taylor pulled the edges of her coat a bit closer, aware of her near nakedness beneath as the wool brushed against her overheated skin.

"Hi, Harry."

Harry Fontain had already cornered her elbow and was leading her inside, giving her no choice but to follow. But then, wasn't this why she'd come?

Harry scanned the bar. "Can't see him. Maybe he's out back. Want me to check?"

"No!" Taylor caught his hand. "I mean, not right now. Leave him be. I thought I might um..." She spied the pool table. "How about a game of pool?"

"You play?" Harry seemed surprised, but then so was she. She didn't a have a clue how to play.

"Sure. I was brought up on the game," she lied. "Come on, how about a little one-on-one?"

"That's basketball."

"Pardon?"

"One-on-one is basketball."

"Oh." Damn. And she thought she'd been so clever. "Never mind, you get my drift."

"Sure thing."

Taylor eyed the pool green with suspicion. The only time she'd tried the game, she'd ended up sending the pool cue through the green and been ordered out of the youth club.

"So, who starts?"

"Better take off your coat. This is going to be a hot game."

He didn't know the half of it. Taylor undid the last button and let Harry lift the coat from her shoulders.

"Wowee. Does Cade know what you're wearing?"

"Should he?" She turned and flashed a bright smile over her shoulder toward Harry. The man's expression turned crimson. "Let's play, Harry." She picked up the cue stick, aware that as she circled the table, every man in the room eyed her from top to toe. The leather shorts rose up her rear, and she would swear the waistcoat had shrunken. Her breasts were almost popping out. With as much composure as she could muster, she tried to wiggle her breasts back in place without drawing too much attention.

Failed on that score.

Harry and his cohorts exhaled a collective breath of beer-tainted air.

Being ogled didn't feel great. In fact, Taylor almost turned tail and ran. But she was on a mission. One last shot.

She bent over the table, aware the shorts rode up even farther and her cleavage was on view for the nine o'clock news. She tried to remember what she'd seen on *Pot Black*.

"That's an idea." She hesitated, the cue tucked under one arm. She flicked a strand of hair back from her face and eyed Harry. "How about a bet?"

"What ya got in mind?"

Yeah. What? From the corner of her eye, she saw Cade walk into the bar from the back room. He looked haggard, as if he hadn't slept for days.

Good job. Neither had she. Now she intended to give him another sleepless night, something to think about—hopefully.

He's the One

"I win, you give me a ride on that Harley I heard you bought last week."

"Sure." Harry looked mighty confident. "And if I win?"

Taylor's gaze shifted fleetingly toward the bar and Cade, lips curving in a slight smile. "Oh, that's easy. How about I give you a kiss?" And she gave Harry her best smile, making sure Cade heard her every word.

Poor Harry. The man's eyes nearly popped out of his head.

"What the hell are you doing here, Taylor?"

"It's a bar, isn't it?"

Cade grabbed Taylor's arm, but his gaze fixated on her breasts, more than visible above the deep V of the buttoned leather waistcoat. Skin he'd kissed.

"Shit," he bit out. "Dressed like that, is what I mean."

She batted her lashes at him. Damn, they were long. Too long. Too seductive. Adrenaline and arousal kicked in, his erection making him instantly uncomfortable.

"Having fun, Cade darling," Taylor purred. "Doing what you said I should and catching up on four years." She trailed a scarlet talon down the center of his T-shirt.

Cade gritted his teeth. He wanted her. Bad. Real bad. "Not here you're not."

"You kicking me out?" She smiled at him. Teasing him. She knew it, and he knew it.

Harry Fontain edged forward. "I'll go with you."

"Keep out of this, Harry. This is between Taylor and I."

"Taylor and me," she corrected sweetly.

"Stop doing that."

"What?" Her eyes widened with feigned innocence.

"That! With those lashes of yours."

"You mean this?" As she blinked several times, a soft peal of fluttery laughter escaped her ruby red lips. Her wide smile bared her teeth—teeth she'd used on him, nipping him.

Oh, hell. He was definitely in deep trouble.

"A girl can go out and have a drink with friends."

"And these are your friends?"

Cade glanced around. Harry, Roger, Ted Samson. The usual crowed hovered around, all eager to see what was going on. He bristled at their intrusion.

"They are, actually." She nodded toward them before returning her direct gaze at him, challenging his sanity. "Any problems?"

He pulled her closer and his grip on her arm tightened. "This isn't the sort of place for you."

"Why not?" she taunted. "What's wrong with it? It's a good bar, pleasant company. Besides, you own it, so I'm safe, aren't I?"

"You tell him, Taylor."

Cade shot the interloper a scathing glance.

"Point one to me, I think." She smiled, running a hand through her long hair. A silken strand brushed against Cade's cheek, and he stilled.

Memories.

Taylor's hair brushed across his sex-dampened skin, trailing over him as she licked him, teased him into oblivion.

Damn, this was hard. More than hard. It was pure torture. "This isn't a game, Taylor."

"No. It's life, and I'm living it, just as you said I should."

She blinked again and smiled sweetly at him. Sweet. Hell, it was temptation and agony all rolled into one.

"It seems to me you don't want to share. I wonder why that is?"

Cade couldn't believe it. Come midnight, Taylor had beaten every guy in the room at pool. Mind you, most of them couldn't see the balls for ogling Taylor. She looked hot. Too hot for them.

Cade eyed the clock above the bar. "Closing time, folks."

"Five minutes to go," Harry called.

"Forget it, Harry. Time's up. Everyone out."

Grumbles aside, Cade hustled everyone out. Taylor walked to the door, her coat draped over her arm.

"Not you."

"I beg your pardon?"

"So you should. You've given me a hard-on all night, and probably every other man in the room too."

She smiled—that sweet, innocent look again. Sweet nothing. Tonight, Taylor was sex on heels, and he wanted to kiss her over and over until he could expunge her from his brain and his body.

"I need a drink. Fancy a nightcap?"

"Sure." Dropping her coat on a nearby chair, Taylor followed him to the bar. "You know, this is all your fault," she said, propping herself up on a barstool.

"You reckon?"

"Absolutely. You helped me *find myself.*"

"Good ol' me. Mr. Helpful."

"Mm." She took a sip of the French blackcurrant liqueur,

smiling up at him through those blasted lashes again. His body heat skidded past boiling.

"Maybe I should set myself up as a shrink."

"Why won't you talk about your past, Cade?"

He skulled the remainder of his beer before answering. "Some memories aren't worth remembering."

"If you don't deal with it, it'll haunt you."

A cracked laugh rumbled from his chest. "You trying to analyze me again? Thought we'd passed that phase."

"Oh, I've passed the lot. But you, you're still back in the past."

"How do you figure that, sweetheart?" he said, trying for nonchalance but coming up empty. He cared. But didn't want to. Caring that much hurt like hell.

"How about some music?" Taylor gestured toward the jukebox.

"Sure."

Still switched on, the garish lights zinged in the dimmed room. Cade poured them both another drink, swallowing back half of his in one gulp. He needed it.

The sultry sounds of a blues number echoed around the room. Cade grabbed their glasses and walked over to Taylor. "Your drink, madam."

She smiled, but didn't move. "Thank you."

"For?"

"Everything."

Cade's throat thickened. "Ms. Sullivan," he said, virtually holding his breath, "would you care to dance?"

Taylor's nod was almost imperceptible, but it was the only encouragement he needed. He took her hand in his, spikes of desire ripping through him with vicious need at the first touch. He gritted his teeth. *It's over. Remember that.*

Yet it didn't feel over. It felt like it had just begun.

Effortlessly, Taylor stepped into his embrace and moved to the rhythmic chords of the music. "How is it that we know each other so intimately, yet I don't know what music you like?"

"I'm easy to please," she said, smiling.

"Easy? Never that, Taylor. You're sweet, hard working."

"And out of here?"

"What?"

Taylor pulled herself from his embrace, snatching herself away, hugging her arms around her chest.

That same old action again. He'd come to recognize it as the moment when she shut down, turned away from him.

Damn. Cade sucked in a deep breath and found his gazed fixed firmly and definitely below her shoulders. The way she folded her arms did sort of squishy, sexy things to her breasts so that they rose above neckline of her vest.

Very enticing. And hell, it made him *very* horny.

Taylor took a few steps back, scouring the room for her bag. "I can't do this."

"You keep saying that, then you come back," Cade countered.

"I know. I'm sorry. It's just that you made me realize what my past has done. It stifled me. Now I want to live, to experience love, marriage and babies and the whole white picket fence thing. You don't want that."

Nope. No way. "It only leads to heartache."

"Hearts ache no matter what, Cade. I might not have much experience in life, but believe me, I know that's a definite."

"Yeah, but I've lived it, seen it first hand. People think they love someone, get married, then it falls flat. Lust and love get confused."

"Well, that's something you should know. You sure as hell know lust."

"We both do. That's why we're good together. We understand lust."

"But that's it. Together for how long? What future is there in that? As you say, lust doesn't last. Then where would we be?"

Yeah, where? Cade's gut zinged and every damned part of him ached as he watched Taylor shut herself off from him, her lowered lashes shadowing her thoughts.

Realization made his chest tighten. This was it. She was leaving, and he'd probably never see her again. She didn't want him anymore. She'd used him for her own needs. But now it was over.

Just like his ex-girlfriend Angie and his mother. See—use and leave.

He could do "over". He could. Cade reached for another drink and slugged it back. "Bye, Taylor."

"Damn. Damn. Damn. This wasn't how it was meant to go." Taylor thought she'd planned for every eventuality, that she could tempt him. Obviously she wasn't woman enough for him, even in less clothing than a Barbie doll. But as these thoughts crowded her brain, Taylor realized it was she who'd pulled back. She who'd stopped dancing. Okay, so he'd said goodbye, but she'd been running hot and cold. Wanting him, teasing him with the sleazy outfit. Now she was running scared.

Again.

"Sorry, Cade, got to go. Wedding tomorrow." She gathered up her coat then quickly shucked it on before he could reach her. She turned to him, willing the fresh tremors that threatened to leave her in a heap at his feet to dissolve.

"I…I," she stuttered. "How do I say thank you?"

"You just did," he said. But there wasn't a bit of humor in his expression.

"It doesn't seem enough. You've given me a new start," she said. One she now knew she didn't want to go alone but had to. Cade had to make his own decisions, his own path in life. Taylor swallowed hard, trying to clear a suddenly blocked airway. "Take care, Cade. You'll be a success. Good luck." She wrenched the door open and tottered into the dark, lonely night before she allowed herself to think. But thinking hurt.

"Why does love hurt so much?" Sitting in her office the next morning after zero sleep, Taylor hugged a cushion to her chest. Through eyes that stung, gritty and tear-filled, she looked up at the concerned face of Nita.

"I suppose that's what makes it worthwhile," Nita said and replenished Taylor's third cup of straight black coffee. She passed the mug, which she gratefully accepted. She took a draught of piping hot liquid, hoping it would cheer her up.

"Maybe a hit of double caffeine will bring me back to life," she mused, trying to dig herself out of a stupor. "How can it be worthwhile if the other person doesn't figure it out?"

"I don't know, Taylor. I'm sorry."

Taylor blinked back another bout of tears. "Yeah, me too."

"But at least you can answer those sex questions now."

"Yeah, orgasms, vaginismus or how big is big?" she said,

grinning despite herself. Her eyes lowered as memories of Cade holding her, his fingers exploring and lips kissing her, washed over her. It was too much and, for the umpteenth time in forty-eight hours, tears began.

Nita plunked herself down beside Taylor. "That's right. Cry. Let it all out."

"How long, Nita? How long until it gets better?"

"A while."

Left to her own sadness, Taylor mulled over what Nita had said. *A while.* She hoped so, but right now it felt like it was forever. It hurt. Deep down inside, where she'd never let anyone in. Until now. Till Cade Harper.

"Big mistake."

Chapter Fourteen

"You are one fool, Cade."

The pile of accounts Cade had been working on fell from his hands to his already overcrowded desk. He stood and scowled. "Get out of here, Zane."

"Not until I've given you a piece of my mind."

Cade gritted his teeth. "Do I have to listen?"

"If you know what's good for you." Zane thrust him back into his seat. "Now sit there and keep that trap shut, brother."

"Get it over with quick." Cade eyed the blueprints scattered over his desk. His dream project. But not his real-life dream. That space had been taken. He choked back an oath and squashed that thought. "I've got to see the builders at the new site," he informed his brother, ever hopeful Zane would turn tail and walk right out of his office.

"Yeah, and isn't that just convenient. Business and more business. What else is there?"

"Exactly." Cade folded his arms across his chest.

"Life? Love? Have you heard of those words?"

"I'm in no mood to listen to your ramblings."

"Haven't been in any mood since Taylor walked out on you," his brother cut in. "Now why would that be?"

A heavy sigh slid past Cade's grim, downturned mouth. He

eyed his brother. So like himself, yet very different. "You may be my brother, but right now I want to punch your lights out."

Zane chuckled and flexed his fingers. "Bring it on."

A familiar smile spread across Zane's face and, for a split second, fear knotted in Cade's gut. He shoved his chair back and stood. Zane was tall, but he was taller.

"Don't try and intimidate me, Cade. Won't work. Hasn't since I hit thirteen," Zane said as walked to the door that connected to the bar and opened it. "You're my big brother. I look up to you. I *used* to think you knew everything. I guess I was wrong." He shrugged. "You've got to work this out for yourself, mate."

"There's nothing to work out," Cade said flatly.

Zane made a clicking noise with his tongue. "Now that's *definitely* where you're wrong. So I'll say goodbye. Happy analyzing."

Zane stepped through the door and closed it behind him, but just as the latch went to click, he popped his head back around the door. "One more thing. Our mother left because Dad didn't care enough. Do you care enough?"

And with that, the door shut with a resounding click, leaving Cade alone—finally—to think. Something he was very uncomfortable doing.

Sleep again proved elusive, and Cade tossed and turned as the hours ticked by until he heard the birds' first call and daybreak tipped over the conical peak of Rangitoto Island in the harbor.

"Bloody birds. Shut up," he snarled and dragged his pillow from the bed and slammed it down on his head, hoping to drown out the birdsong.

But it was no use. Nothing worked. The still-strong autumn sun had long ago beaten a path through his bedroom window, and the birds were now in full chorus. He gave up, giving them a scowl as he hauled his sorry butt toward the shower.

Maybe that would clear his head and lighten his mood.

"Not damn likely," he grumbled as the full force of the shower hit him.

He stayed under the pulsing jet spray until the water turned frigid, then snapped off the faucet and exited the shower, toweled dry and dressed.

Thank God it was Sunday. At least he'd get some peace and quiet from the regulars. Their incessant questioning about Taylor's whereabouts was driving him nuts, and the fact that he couldn't answer them made it a hundred times worse.

What was he going to do? Give up?

After his third strong, black coffee, loaded with caffeine, Cade thought perhaps he could face work, so he headed downstairs to the back room and his computer.

"Work is what I need." He grimaced as he eyed the piles of unopened mail. What was wrong with him? He thrived on work, on getting it done. Yet here it was unopened for days.

An hour later, the pile hadn't diminished, and he'd achieved zilch.

"Come on, Harper, get it together." He grabbed the nearest pile and began sorting through it, but hadn't done more than the first couple of accounts when a thunderous knock resounded on the side door of the premises.

Cade ignored it. Maybe they'd go away. But it continued, louder and more insistent with every thunderous rap.

"Damn it, it's Sunday," he snarled as he wrenched back the

bolt and opened the door. "Hugh?"

"Gotta talk, Cade. Gotta figure it out." Hugh Prendergast didn't wait to be asked in, but barged past Cade and headed straight through to the bar. He grabbed a tumbler and punched it under the whiskey nozzle three times, filling his glass. Cade watched as his normally staid best friend downed the contents in one unbroken guzzle, then replenished it before turning to face him.

"You don't look too good, mate," he said to Hugh, which was an understatement. With black circles shadowing sleep deprived, blurry eyes, Hugh looked like death. Stubble grazed his chin, and his normally dapper appearance was overshadowed by clothes in which he'd obviously slept.

Hugh emptied his second whiskey and set the glass back on bar before speaking. "Same could be said about you."

Cade paused and eyed his reflection in a nearby window. Day old growth, bleary eyes. Yep, he looked a wreck. He turned back to Hugh. "Where's Brianna?"

"We've argued. It's over."

His jaw dropped. "You're joking."

Hugh sank into the chair behind Cade, dropping his head into his hands. "Wish I was." His red-rimmed eyes glistened.

This was serious.

"I should have been like you."

"What do you mean? You love Brianna."

"I know, and I do. But, oh, hell." Hugh let out a few blue expletives, and Cade winced. Hugh didn't swear. Hugh was the good boy, always in control. Knew where he was going, loved Brianna from the moment he set eyes on her.

Just like me and Taylor.

Shut up! Cade refused to listen to his inner ramblings. They didn't matter. Taylor wasn't interested.

"Look, phone her. I'm sure it's okay. New marriages always have blips."

"*You* reckoned marriage wasn't worth it. You're right. It's not."

"You don't mean that," Cade said, shocked at Hugh's despondency.

"Why not? You do."

"Yeah, but... Look, Hugh. I'm not the marrying kind, but you are."

"What about that new woman...Taylor? Katie said you're hot for her."

"Katie should mind her own business. Besides, she's got a thing going with...ah, someone else," Cade informed his friend. "A dead guy."

Hugh's shock was obvious. "Hell, tough opposition."

"You're telling me. How the hell do I compete with a dead guy?"

For a few seconds, Cade was lost in his own misery, then he shook his head and focused on his best friend. "Come on. Leave that drink. I think coffee's on order. Strong and black. Then maybe you'll be able to think straight." Cade hit the kitchen, switching on the kettle and getting a couple of coffee mugs from the cupboard. The irony of what he offered Hugh as a medicine for his marital woes wasn't lost on Cade, considering the vast quantity of coffee he'd used to drown his sorrows the last few days.

"So what went wrong with Taylor?"

"A one night stand. That's all." He shrugged, knowing it was absolutely nothing like it.

"I would say there's more to it than that, by the look of

you," Hugh said as he took his cup of coffee from Cade.

Tendrils of white steam spiraled from Cade's coffee. He stared at it for brief moment. "Nah. Nothing else. It's over."

He took several draughts of his coffee, eyes closing momentarily as he let the hot liquid revive him. No sleep. No concentration, and now Hugh on his doorstep wallowing in marriage dramas. What else?

"She dumped you!" Hugh spluttered into his coffee. "The woman dumped you. My God, I can't believe it."

The pulse in Cade's throat skittered, and his jaw clenched. "It happens," he said, trying for nonchalance, while inside his gut churned. It hurt. He couldn't believe how much it hurt. And it shouldn't. Letting it hurt made it way too close to home. Too close to his past, and he wasn't about to let his past hurt impinge on the present. Cade definitely didn't want to care. Caring hurt.

"She doesn't answer my calls," he finally admitted.

"Think she's trying to tell you something?"

"Loud and clear." Cade reached for his coffee and gulped back the remainder.

"And the problem is?" Hugh prompted.

"The problem is, mate, I feel like I've been shafted."

"Women don't shaft you. You're the guy that loves and leaves 'em."

Yep. The truth hurt. This was a different truth, however, and one he didn't want to face. He was determined to change the way this conversation was going. "Your wife loves you, Hugh. You love her. It's as simple as that."

"Good deflection."

Cade offered his friend a sheepish grin.

How come it sounded simple for everyone else when his life

was a disaster area? Zane had said his mother left because of their father. But she didn't just leave dear old dad. She left him, Zane and Katie too. What about them?

"Brianna told me to go," Hugh said, breaking into Cade's morose miasma.

"Why?"

"Says I'm married to my job, not to her."

"Oh..."

"What do you mean, oh?"

"That's big stuff for a woman."

"And you should know. You've had plenty of them."

"Low blow, Hugh."

Hugh dragged a hand through is carrot-top curls. "Yeah, I'm sorry."

"Don't worry about it. I've got a tough hide. Look, buy her some flowers, some chocolates. But most of all, go home. Tell her you love her, run the bath for her, give her a foot massage, anything that tells her you appreciate her. Work is important, I'm the first one to agree on that one, but you're a team now. You can't spend twenty-four/seven hunched over a computer program anymore."

"Yeah, I know you're right."

Cade smiled at his friend. They'd been through a lot. It was good to be able to help him. "So what are you doing here?" Cade pushed himself away from the bench and strode toward the door with Hugh following.

"You sure you're okay about Taylor?" Hugh asked.

Cade wasn't about to let his friend start up on that again. "Don't worry about me."

Hugh eyed him with that steel gray gaze of his, the one Cade had seen him use when trying to suss out some computer programming glitch. "You've changed."

"Enough," he said and gave Hugh a playful push. "Go home. Love her like there's no tomorrow."

Cade stood at his door and watched Hugh walk the short path from the side exit to his car. All the while his own advice rang hollow in his ears—and continued to ring long after Hugh had departed to make amends with his bride.

Hugh had accused him of changing.

He had.

The trouble was, Cade wasn't sure he wanted change or what to do about it. It scared the hell out of him. But there was something else that scared him more—something exciting and new and very tempting.

The lights of the jukebox blinked a kaleidoscope of colors. Standing in front of it, Cade searched for one particular song, found it and punched the button. The soft whirring of electronics clicked into gear and the song started. Soft and gentle and full of memories. Memories not yet twenty-four hours old, though they haunted him as if they were as old as time.

Do you care—enough?

She didn't want to think about the setting, though it was the perfect spot for a wedding.

Just not hers. Not here. Or anywhere, for that matter.

The dread in Taylor's stomach knotted, and she had to steady herself. She loved Cade. He just didn't love her, couldn't let go of his abandonment issues long enough to trust in the present.

But Greta Peters and Erueti Nathan were going to love their

He's the One

wedding. It was everything they'd ever wanted and then some. That little bit extra had been Taylor's idea.

Her visions, her dreams.

Today she was giving her dreams away.

May had given way to June, and the crisp air hung fresh, the sky a cloudless blue. In the garden bordering the drive to the church entrance, early blossoms poked through damp ground, their fragrance scenting the air.

It was beautiful. Everything was set. She surveyed her work. Bouquets of rose buds lined the altar, and the golds, pinks and blues of the stained glass windows glittered like jewels and lit the grand old church.

Taylor smiled. She'd done well. Her couple's fantasy wedding would come true.

"I can't believe it." Hair flying in her wake, Nita scurried down the aisle toward her. "Have you got the French ribbon? The four-inch wide with golden angels?"

"Of course, in here." Taylor scrambled in her emergency box, but came up empty. "It was. I know I put in here. I *never* forget things."

"Tell that to the good luck fairy." Nita's worry lines deepened. "This hasn't been your week for luck. Your mind is elsewhere."

Taylor straightened and rubbed her suddenly damp palms down the sides of her dress. "Not now, Nita. I..."

"You've been preoccupied by a hunk."

"No!" She gripped her bag with white-knuckle intensity, but knew her denial to be futile.

Nita rested a hand on her shoulder. "It's okay. You're allowed to love. Rob wouldn't want you to still grieve."

"I'm..." But Taylor couldn't finish the sentence. Did Nita

think she pined for her dead fiancé? How far from the truth could she be? She hadn't loved Rob, like she should have. And that was why she couldn't trust herself now. She loved Cade. But she couldn't give herself to someone who didn't want her.

One day, when she had thought Rob asleep and sat at his bedside, the tears had come and she wept for the *liking* she had mistaken for *love*.

But Rob had woken and, in that fleeting moment when the subconscious fights with the conscious, she'd seen the comprehension in his eyes. He knew her lies.

And she'd seen his hurt too.

But he never said anything and had died with the hurt inside, leaving Taylor with the guilt.

"I won't crawl, Nita. Cade needs to figure out that he is himself and not a product of a marriage disaster, nor is it a predetermination for his own."

"My, you have been digging deep."

"I had a phone call from his brother Zane, that's all."

"And Zane filled you in on the psyche of Cade?"

"Something like that," she agreed, not really wanting to tell Nita the whole story.

Cade blamed his mother for leaving his father, but in fact his father's drinking had started the process long ago. But when she left, she had nowhere to go, no one to turn to, no way to take her children with her. However, Cade blamed his mother for abandoning him and to this day lived his life by what he perceived as her mistake.

And now she and Cade were the victims of everyone's lies and truths and hurts.

With Nita offering to save the day and racing back for the angel ribbon, Taylor paced the church, glancing at her watch every few seconds. Why was it when disaster struck, time seemed to stand still?

"Taylor?"

Cade rested against the arched doorway to the church. He looked good. Tired. Beautiful. Taylor's heart did a triple flip. She wanted so much to love him. "What are you doing here?"

"Not 'Hello, Cade. Nice to see you'?" he quipped.

She willed herself to remain calm, balling her hands at her sides when what she really wanted to do was run them through his hair, hold him and kiss him—a lot. "You look good. New outfit?" His gaze lowered slowly, teasing over each curve. His lips were pursed as if he was deciding something. "Where have the gray suits all gone? Do they have a suit heaven?"

Taylor found herself pulling at the hem of the dress she wore. Nita had said it was okay. It felt far too short.

"The suits weren't *that* bad."

He gave her a sort of quirky smile. "Yes, they were. They covered you neck to knee, hiding the real Taylor Sullivan."

"So is this better?" she asked, unsure why she actually wanted his approval.

With sparkling glints in his eyes, Cade appraised her.

Nothing had changed. The same old temptation, the quirky good boy versus bad boy that had hooked her in the first place.

"Turn around."

"What?"

"I said turn around and give me a twirl."

Taylor erupted into a fit of giggles. "You're joking. We're in a church."

He glanced over his shoulder toward the closed wooden doors. "There's just us two. So how about you show off your new dress."

"I...simply went shopping, that's all." She hesitated, though her voice sounded far more composed than she felt.

"Brave move."

"What do you mean?"

"Whoa, don't get all sparky. Although I do remember a mighty fine spark a few nights back, Ms. Sullivan."

Taylor grabbed his elbow and spun him away from the altar. "Your soul will be damned in the flames of hell if you talk of that in this church."

He shrugged. "Already halfway there. At least it seems so the last few days," he said cryptically. "New make-up, and you smell good too," he said, dropping his head to hers and inhaling her perfume. "Sweet scented lilacs. Just like my granny used to grow."

Taylor's jaw dropped. "I didn't know you knew those sorts of things."

"Ah, but that's it. You, Taylor, don't know enough about me, *yet*."

Taylor busied herself with her clipboard and kept her gaze firmly fixed on the page, which wasn't much use as every number blurred and the list of names read like a pile of mumbo jumbo. "Well, this is all very nice, but I'm sorry you can't stay. I've got a wedding to get organized."

"I can't leave yet," Cade said succinctly.

Oh, boy. The revving butterflies in Taylor's belly began their frantic partying once more. "Why not? Are you a guest?" She reread the names on her board. "Oh, God, have I left your name off? What a disaster. The whole week, the ribbons."

"Taylor. It's okay. I'm not a guest. You were going to twirl for me."

"Twirl?" she repeated, struck dumb for a second. "Cade,

you didn't come here just to get me to twirl in a dress. This is ridiculous."

"You're right." He winked at her, dimples denting his tanned cheeks, and when she looked back up at him, his eyes glittered with humor.

"About what?"

But Cade never had the opportunity to answer as a breathless Nita entered from the side vestry waving a giant roll of ribbon. "I've got it. On the desk where you put it before we left," she said, wagging a finger.

Taylor gave Nita a grateful smile and, taking the reel, turned to Cade. "I don't have time to talk now. I have a wedding to finish and not much time left."

"Can I help?"

"You want to help?"

"Yeah, why not? You know, the knight in shining armor to the rescue thing." He grinned.

Don't do that, Taylor screamed silently. *Don't smile, don't tempt me. Please.* She'd only just got herself on an even keel, managed to stem the loneliness.

Who are you trying to kid?

For a moment which seemed to stretch a lifetime, Taylor looked at Cade, from his tousled hair that tipped the collar of his shirt to his unshaven jaw. She remembered the heat that stubble had elicited as his lips had kissed hers, remembered the brush of his hair as it tickled her electrified skin.

"Taylor, they're nearly here," Nita reminded her.

Taylor shot into business mode. "Okay, you're on. I need you."

Never had she ever said a truer word.

"Right, what do I do?"

"Take the ribbon," she said, pointing to the huge reel of ribbon Nita carried. "Start it off at the center point on the rafters and wind down in a spiral. You'll need eight spirals in all to hang to all eight points of the dome."

"Got it."

Cade grabbed the roll and, at a run, snatched the ladder that leant against a pew. He positioned it beneath the center of the dome and scooted up, tack hammer in one hand, the reel in the other, to tack the ribbon in place. "Here's the reel. Start rolling, sweetheart," he said, leaning down to Taylor and passing her the roll.

Working quickly, she unwound the reel so it corkscrewed into a long strand. Once at the far corner, she cut it, and Cade, who'd followed her progress, scooted over and tacked the end of the first spiral in place so that it hung in a gentle sweep from the dome to the walls.

Turning to start the second one, Taylor faltered and came up hard against Cade's chest. She put her hands out to correct her balance, which, along with everything else, could be added to her list of mistakes.

She felt him, all warm and enticing, his breathing uneven. Time slowed, and she lifted her gaze to his.

Nita was right. He was a hunk. Just one look at him and her body fired, desire pooling way down low, sensual memories curling into overdrive. But she knew it was more than that. She loved him. Blast it.

His head dropped toward her.

"See what a good team we make, Taylor? You and me—we can conquer anything."

Taylor's throat closed. She couldn't breathe, couldn't think, couldn't do anything. She wanted him to kiss her. Willed him to. Her heart said please, while her brain warned her.

This was stupid.

This wouldn't work.

He doesn't do permanent and only wants your body.

Grab it. Take it. Forget commitment.

His lips touched hers. Soft and sweet, full of loving and promise and desire. A flutter of a sigh escaped her as she leant into him, wrapped in his arms.

It felt wonderful. Perfect.

"Come on, you two, the other lovers are arriving in a few minutes."

Taylor yanked herself from Cade's arms. "What the hell am I doing?"

"Kissing me." He grinned down at her.

"Making a mistake," she muttered.

Cade's expression hardened, eyes narrowing on her, the golden glints turning brittle.

Without another word, Cade took the reel from her and climbed the ladder another seven times, tacking, unraveling the ribbon, finishing it off and storing the ladder in the tool room at the back of the church before the first guests arrived.

It was all done to perfection minutes later. Taylor stood to one side and watched their expressions as they entered the silver and gold wonderland.

Cade put his arm around her shoulders and gave her a hug. "Looks good."

It took all her effort not to turn and hold him—to kiss him. Keeping her voice steady and warning her insides to behave, she braved the effort of speaking. "I enjoy this part the most. Seeing the surprise and wonder on their faces. It makes it all worthwhile."

"Mm, I can understand that."

Thirty minutes later, the organ crescendoed and the newly married couple turned to the congregation and beamed.

"They look so happy and in love," Cade whispered in her ear.

Taylor jumped. She'd been mesmerized by the ceremony, watching it unfold. But it wasn't Greta and Erueti walking down the aisle, all smiles for family and friends, but her and Cade. She'd envisioned the two of them in place of the happy couple.

Stupid!

Taylor bit back an angry wail. Why do this to herself? She shook her head and turned to Cade as the last of the guests filed out of the church.

"Thanks for your help. How I left that reel of ribbon behind, I don't know."

"I do. Your mind isn't on the job," Nita butted in as she walked past with the priest.

"Sounds just like me," Cade admitted.

"Pardon?"

"Forgetting things. Not concentrating on the job. These last few days have been somewhat, ah... disturbed."

"It was simply a slip up, that's all."

"Taylor, when was the last time you slipped up?" Cade challenged.

"I..."

"See." He smiled. "My point exactly."

"Don't!"

His smile widened. "You mean the dimples?"

She nodded, her embarrassment total. She took a deep breath and held herself rigid so that every part of her ached. But most of all, her heart ached nonstop. "Your shining armor routine worked. Thanks. But I've got to get going. Bye." She hugged her bag to her and tried for nonchalant. Tried calm and controlled, while inside she screamed *fake*. Inside she was all twisted and torn and hurting and just wanting to get the hell out of there, far away from Cade so she could start again.

"Going anywhere special?"

"That isn't any business of yours, Cade."

He lifted one dark eyebrow, grinning wider.

Blast him.

"Well, it is, just a little."

"I beg your pardon?"

"You beg me a lot, Ms. Sullivan. I quite like that." Cade took a few steps toward her, closing the gap. An edgy heat zinged between them.

Taylor bit down hard on her bottom lip. "Purely a figure of speech," she said waspishly.

"Perhaps, but I rather fancy the thought of you begging me."

"When hell freezes over."

"Sounds hot and sexy."

"In your dreams," she countered. Taylor scanned the church. Her dreams. All that work, the beauty of the flowers and fragrance, the ribbons. All for a moment in time. She only hoped it created the memories the couple wanted.

"That's just the problem, sweetheart. You're in my dreams. All the time. In fact you are my dream."

"I don't want to hear this, Cade. Don't do the 'I need you, now let's get down and dirty' routine."

"Sounds intriguing."

Taylor stalled him, putting her hand up as he went to

touch her. "Sounds like too much danger. I can't do danger anymore. It doesn't last." *And it hurts too much.*

"You wanted to, though."

She couldn't fight any longer. "Yes, I did, and you know exactly the reason why I did what I did."

The humorous light in Cade's eyes flicked off, and they darkened to a quiet seriousness.

"And as I said before, I felt privileged." As the last guests filed past, giving them curious glances, Cade pulled her toward him, turning them both away from prying eyes.

With the church emptied, the sound of their voices carried across the vacant space and high into the rafters, mingling with the sparkling ribbon and the golden angels.

Cade shrugged. "I couldn't figure it out at first," he said.

"Figure what?"

"Why I had an intense urge to protect you. It's a big bad world out there, and you, believe it or not, put me in a difficult situation."

"Yeah, right. Like which day, where, when?"

"No, that wasn't it at all. It's weird, but even in this day and age, I felt a certain responsibility. You were upset when we sort of…ah, started and stopped."

"Doesn't give a girl great confidence if the guy keeps having second thoughts."

"Okay. I admit, part of me wanted to run a mile. Get out while I could. The other part." He grinned and trailed his fingers down her bare arms. "That part knew I couldn't leave even if I wanted to. I was hooked from the moment you walked in. You know when I said you were teaching me?"

A volley of expectation skipped across Taylor's heart. Unable to find her voice, she nodded. She wanted to hope, to pray, but it proved too hard.

"You were teaching me to care, sweetheart."

Taylor lifted a hand to his cheek. She wanted to brush away the ache she saw etched in his eyes, ease his pain and hurt. He brought her hand to his lips. "You're special, Taylor."

Her eyes widened, tears welling.

"Yes, you are," he repeated, dotting a kiss on the tip of her nose. He pulled back and it seemed as if all her breath exhaled in one long whoosh, holding her hopes and love and every heart-felt dream she'd ever had.

"I've gone through my life trying not to care," Cade continued. "When my mother took off without a backward glance, I said it didn't matter. I was wrong. It did."

"But she had problems," Taylor said, coming to his mother's defense.

"So big she couldn't come back for us? Perhaps." He shrugged. "Zane found her in some tenement in Sydney. She's been through several husbands since. But it doesn't change the past. And that past left me believing caring was too hard."

"And now?"

"When you said goodbye, I was angry. Angry because you left."

"But we had a deal."

"I know. Mostly though, I was angry with myself because I was too scared. I hurt like hell and wanted to renegotiate the terms."

"On your terms only, though. You wanted me in your bed."

"A good place to be." He grinned. His lips covered hers.

Taylor tasted him. It felt familiar. Real. And wonderful. She wanted him so very badly. Just as she had that night in the bar, dressed in her biker gear. Showing him what he was going to miss.

"Life was easier if I hardened my heart and was the one to call the shots and say goodbye."

"Except it didn't work this time."

"No. I'm sorry I hurt you. Insinuating you were only good enough for part time was hurtful, but you leaving made me think about what I was losing. And, Ms. Sullivan, I'm not prepared to lose you. Commitment means being together. I want us to be together."

Taylor's fingers brushed over Cade's lips.

"Can you forgive me for being a jerk? I should have known and recognized it from the get-go, but, well...I was blind."

"Should have known what?"

"That you were different. You were the one."

"Oh, Cade." Taylor snuggled into him, delighting in the feel of his arms as they tightened around her. She felt warm and safe. That's what Cade was. A safe haven. The man she loved.

Cade looked down at her. "You have me wrapped around your finger. I love you, Taylor Sullivan. I love you so much it hurts. We're linked, Taylor. Forever."

Just then a commotion echoed from outside the church, and Cade slapped his head. "My surprise. You, madam, made me forget."

"What surprise? Spill the beans."

"Not telling."

"Spoilsport." Taylor's voice turned into laughter as he raced her outside and into the alley beside the church. There, in its splendid glory, was the Lincoln convertible. Taylor stalled, suddenly suspicious. "Are you suggesting I go for a ride with you?"

"Yes. No, well, not right now. Later, definitely later."

"Last time I was in one of your cars, Cade, we ended up having sex."

He winked. "So we did."

"Are you asking me to have sex with you in the car?"

Cade shifted from foot to foot, an impish grin curving his mouth. "Sounds good, but no, that's not actually the surprise. Come on." He tugged on her hand and led her toward the car. The closer they got, the louder the noise became.

A dog noise. Barking. Loud and very high pitched.

"You've got a dog in that car."

Cade nodded, and Taylor looked to the car, peering in through the window at the yapping frenzy of fluffy white and brown fur, and back to Cade. "But this is your pride and joy."

"No, it's not. You take that title. And just to prove it, I got Milly for you. All married couples have dogs before they start on the human kind. Kids," he said, beaming.

"Dogs, kids. Married?" Taylor shouted the last word.

"Yes. Married. I want to marry you, Taylor. I want you in my bed, beside me every day and night for the next millennium."

"Does Milly have to join us?"

"Nope—she's purely at the end of the bed."

"Then it's a deal. You, me, four classic cars and Milly. Sounds like a good start to a family."

"Sweetheart, it sounds just right, as long as that sexy underwear stays."

"Oh...absolutely."

About the Author

To learn more about Jane Beckenham, please visit www.janebeckenham.com/. Send an email to Jane at neiljane@ihug.co.nz.

*When a good man is hard to find,
there's only one thing left to do. Buy one.*

My Gigolo
© *2010 Molly Burkhart*

As far as Gabrielle is concerned, her life isn't at all a mess. It's simply taught her a hard lesson—never rely on anyone else for her own happiness. It's not that she's against having sex. Far from it. It's just that if it comes with strings tied to the word "love", she'll pass.

Now if only she could stop her sister and friends from trying to show her the error of her solitary ways. Especially after their latest trick—hiring a male prostitute for her birthday.

In all his time as a male escort, Jack's never met anyone as intriguing as down-to-earth Gabe. Or as determined to refuse his charms. She has no idea whom she's dealing with, though. Jack's a consummate professional in all aspects of his chosen field. Including coercion.

One minute, Gabe is agreeing to a night of no-strings sex. The next, she's staring up at a man who turns her body and soul inside out. Jack is staring down at a woman he can't imagine never seeing again. Both are suddenly aware there are only two ways this could end: a match made in heaven…or sheer disaster.

Warning: Explicit sex, illegal sexual practices, zombies, a clown, and the strangest minigolf course ever conceived.

Available now in ebook and print from Samhain Publishing.

GREAT CHEAP FUN

Discover eBooks!

THE FASTEST WAY TO GET THE HOTTEST NAMES

Get your favorite authors on your favorite reader, long before they're out in print! Ebooks from Samhain go wherever you go, and work with whatever you carry—Palm, PDF, Mobi, Kindle, nook, and more.

WWW.SAMHAINPUBLISHING.COM